Relationships & Us

Stories from Everyday Life

MOHAMMAD HASAN

Prologue

Relationships & Us is a collection of stories inspired by the quiet moments and everyday encounters we all experience in our lives. These are not grand tales of adventure or sweeping dramas, but rather reflections of the subtle, often unnoticed dynamics that shape our relationships with the people around us. Each story in this collection explores a different facet of human connection—how seemingly simple relationships, when looked at more closely, reveal a depth of complexity and emotion that is easy to overlook. It aims to explore the quiet, latent emotions that people carry within themselves. Some emotions are suppressed, some are hidden behind smiles, and others remain unacknowledged even to the person feeling them. It's these concealed layers of human experience that give depth to relationships and make each individual's journey unique. At its core, *Relationships & Us* is about people—ordinary people who could be you, me, or anyone we encounter in our day-to-day lives. It's about the ways we relate to each other, the invisible threads that bind us, and the misunderstandings that tear us apart. Through these stories, we see how human relationships are never as simple as they seem, and how, in the end, they are what define us as individuals.

Contents

Baigan ka Bharta

1

"Farhan, could you please help me with the straightener?" Mahin asked softly, her voice carrying a mix of trust and affection.

"Yes," Farhan replied, taking the straightener from her hand. He positioned it carefully near her hair, his movements gentle and attentive. "Hold it like this, press when I tell you, and then slowly move it in the direction of the slope. Don't press too hard, or it might break a hair or two."

With a delicate concentration, Farhan guided the straightener down the length of Mahin's hair, his fingers brushing against the soft strands. Mahin adjusted the angle of her head slightly, allowing the straightener to glide smoothly.

"Just a bit to the right," she murmured, barely above a whisper, "and gently pushed it down. Yes, like that. Thanks."

Farhan carefully released the straightener, watching with a hint of amusement as Mahin took over, her hands skillfully adding the finishing touches. As she worked, she glanced up, catching his eye in the mirror. A soft smile formed on her lips, warmed by his presence. Farhan stood behind her, his gaze tender and unwavering, clearly captivated by this quiet, everyday intimacy. She felt his love in the soft silence that filled the room, his presence a comforting constant in her life.

"Farhan, Mahin, are you ready? We're already running late!" Farhan's mother called from downstairs, her voice echoing through the house.

"Coming, Maa," Farhan replied, his voice faint but just loud enough to be heard below.

"Farhan, please give me back my comb! We're already late, and Maa will get upset if we take more than five minutes," Mahin pleaded, her tone a mix of frustration and urgency. Farhan, however, only grinned mischievously, holding the comb high above his head, just out of Mahin's reach.

"Farhan, stop!" she said, a playful irritation in her voice as she jumped up, trying to grab the comb. But he kept it just out of reach, enjoying the moment.

"Please, give it back," Mahin said, her tone becoming more serious as she looked up at him.

"Okay, okay, don't get angry," Farhan said, his smile softening as he handed over the comb with an apologetic grin.

Mahin snatched it back, her exasperation melting into a reluctant smile, unable to stay upset with him for long.

2

"Oh, what a beautiful daughter-in-law you have, Mrs. Gauhar. I'm already envious!" remarked Mrs. Usha, her eyes sparkling with admiration.

"And I must say, Farhan, you're a very lucky young man," she continued. "You should be grateful to have such a wonderful wife in Mahin."

Farhan gave a shy smile, his cheeks warming under the praise. Mahin blushed deeply, glancing first at Farhan, then back at Mrs. Usha, a soft smile spreading across her face.

Farhan's mother forced a smile in response, nodding politely at Mrs. Usha's compliment, though a hint of reluctance lingered in her expression.

"But Aunty, my brother is also a gem of a person," Zehra chimed in, unable to hold back. "He takes such good care of Bhabhi. Even after a long day at work, he helps her with chores and often serves her bed tea in the morning."

"Stop it, Zehra, this isn't the right occasion," Farhan whispered, clearly embarrassed.

"Why, Bhai? Haven't you told everyone that you were the one who taught Bhabhi how to make the perfect traditional Dum Chai?" Zehra teased, a mischievous grin spreading across her face.

"Yes, I have, but stop it," Farhan replied, shifting uncomfortably as his cheeks reddened with embarrassment.

"Oh, and what about those shapeless chapatis Bhabhi made?" Zehra continued, her tone becoming even more playful. "You ate every single one without letting anyone else notice, didn't you?"

"God, this girl!" Farhan groaned; his frustration evident as he tried to hide his smile. His embarrassment only deepened, knowing he couldn't escape Zehra's relentless teasing.

"Of course, beta, I've known Farhan since he was a child, and I've always been fond of him," Mrs. Usha responded warmly. "You know, once Pushkar and I even joked about the possibility of him and Garima ending up together. Hahaha," she added, brushing off the topic with a light laugh.

Everyone settled into their seats, the atmosphere thick with anticipation as the bride and groom began to share their vows. Their words were filled with love and commitment, promising not only to cherish each other but above all, to respect one another and protect their emotional well-being. As they spoke, the room fell silent, each guest moved by the depth of the couple's devotion and the sincerity of their promises.

3

"Hello, beta! How are you?" Mrs. Usha exclaimed, her face lighting up as she was greeted by Zehra. "You're looking slimmer, aren't you? Been sticking to those yoga classes?"

"Just a little, Aunty," Zehra replied with a grin. "It's mostly the diet. I'm cutting back on carbs."

"Oh, I could never do that! I'm too much of a foodie," Mrs. Usha chuckled. "All these fitness fads are for you Gen Z folks. We're too old for that!"

"But Aunty, you look younger than ever," Zehra complimented, her eyes twinkling.

Mrs. Usha laughed, her eyes rolling playfully. "Oh, ask your Uncle! He never gives me such nice compliments!"

"Yes, yes, beta," Mr. Prakash interjected with a cheeky grin. "It's her beauty that trapped me all those years ago and still keeps me hooked."

"Oh, is that so, dear?" Mrs. Usha shot back with a raised eyebrow. "We'll see about that when we get back home."

The room filled with laughter as they exchanged playful banter, the warmth of their camaraderie lighting up the space.

"So, 50 years, Gauhar! You and Sabi have come a long way! We still have five years to catch up to you," Mrs. Usha exclaimed, clapping her hands to celebrate the 50th anniversary of Mr. Sabi and Mrs. Gauhar. Her smile was bright, her eyes shining with admiration.

"Maa and Abbu have always been so good together," Zehra added, her voice thick with emotion. "A bond that could never be broken. I'm so proud of them."

"And you should be!" Mrs. Usha chimed in with a nod. "Managing all these years with two kids is no small feat. We could barely manage with Garima & Ravi" She laughed, shaking her head at the memory of her own parenting challenges.

"Farhan," Mrs. Usha turned to him with a playful smile, "you should take a leaf out of their book. You've got a whole lifetime ahead to spend with Mahin, after all."

The guests burst into laughter and Farhan and Mahin blushed shyly.

4

"Try this, Adil. It's Maa's specialty," Farhan said warmly, passing the dish of Chicken do Pyaaza. The rich aroma filled the air as Adil, the youngest of the men, hesitated for a moment before accepting the offering. Prakash Uncle and Naved Sahab were already savoring their servings, murmuring their appreciation between bites.

Meanwhile, Mrs. Gauhar had formed a cozy circle with Mrs. Usha and Mrs. Fatima, their conversation flowing easily over daily chores and shared stories. They sat patiently, waiting for the men to finish their meal, their laughter and chatter a soft backdrop to the dinner.

In the quieter corners of the house, Zehra led Farah to her room with an eager smile. She unveiled her latest creation: a beautifully painted landscape of the Rumi Darwaza, set against the majestic backdrop of the Bada Imambara. The brushstrokes were sharp, neat, and immaculate, capturing every detail with a delicate precision.

Mrs. Usha had proudly managed to get Zehra's paintings displayed at a local exhibition, thanks to the support of "FemForte," a renowned group dedicated to empowering young women to pursue their passions. The group had become a lifeline for many, celebrating and nurturing the talents of young female entrepreneurs, and Zehra's artwork stood as a testament to that spirit of encouragement and achievement.

"Hey, Farhan, come here," Mahin whispered, waving discreetly from the kitchen doorway where only Farhan could see her.

Farhan, unable to hear her clearly, tilted his head and raised an eyebrow in question. Mahin, a little more impatient now, waved again, this time with a hint of playful frustration, urging him to come over.

"You all please continue; I'll just be a couple of minutes," Farhan said to the guests at the table, pushing back his chair gently and standing up. The guests nodded, continuing their conversation, as Farhan made his way into the kitchen.

"Yes, what is it?" he asked, a hint of irritation in his voice at being pulled away from the lively discussion.

"Look at what I made today!" Mahin said, her eyes shining with a mix of excitement and nervousness. She revealed a bowl of perfectly garnished baigan ka bharta, hesitating to bring it out earlier. It was her first time preparing a dish for everyone, and she wasn't sure how it would taste.

"Don't tell me you tried making this!" Farhan exclaimed, surprised.

"Yes! I followed a recipe from Pakeeza Kitchen on YouTube. They explained everything so clearly," she explained, her voice filled with both pride and apprehension.

"Are you sure? Maybe I should taste it first," Farhan offered, reaching for a spoon.

"No! That'll ruin the garnish!" Mahin cried out, quickly covering the bowl with her hands. "Don't worry, I'll serve it myself. I just wanted you to see it before anyone else," she added with a hopeful smile, her excitement bubbling over.

"Okay, let's hope everyone likes it," Farhan said, a hint of uncertainty in his voice, but his expression softened as he saw Mahin's hopeful face.

"Naved Uncle, please try this! I made Baigan ka Bharta especially for the occasion," Mahin said eagerly, placing the dish on the table with a hopeful smile.

Naved Uncle glanced at the bowl, then patted his stomach with a laugh. "Oh, thank you, beta, but I'm too full! Your husband already fed us so well. I think I can only manage a rasgulla for dessert."

Farhan shot Mahin a look, his expression tight with irritation. "Mahin, just leave it here. Everyone will serve themselves," he said, his tone firm as he tried to hide his frustration at her enthusiasm.

Mahin's smile faltered, the joy on her face fading into a look of embarrassment. She nodded, feeling a flush rise in her cheeks, and set the bowl down carefully. With a small, apologetic smile that didn't quite reach her eyes, she quietly retreated back to the kitchen, her heart sinking a little as she stepped away.

"Maa, we've finished dinner and are heading to the lounge now," Farhan announced as he approached the group of ladies engrossed in conversation. "Usha Aunty, Fatima Aunty, please come and enjoy your meal."

"Of course, beta," Mrs. Fatima replied with a warm smile. "The aroma has been making my mouth water! You go ahead and enjoy your time with Adil and the elders."

"Zehra, Farah, if you two are done with your artistic exploration, please join us for dinner!"

"Coming, Maa!" Zehra's voice rang out from the other room.

As the ladies began to settle at the table, Mahin swiftly cleared the used plates and laid out fresh ones, her movements quick and practiced. She smiled at them, making sure everything was perfect.

"Bhabhi, do you need any help?" Zehra called out, appearing in the doorway.

"I'll manage," Mahin replied with a gentle smile. "You take care of Farah."

Zehra nodded, guiding Farah to her seat, while Mahin busied herself with making sure everyone felt welcomed and comfortable.

"Wow, Gauhar, you've still got the flair! This tastes amazing. It's because of people like you that I can never stick to a diet!" exclaimed Mrs. Usha, her eyes twinkling as she took another bite.

"Thank you for the compliment, dear," Mrs. Gauhar replied with a warm smile. "Zehra helped me with the marination and garnishing. She's getting quite good at it."

"These Gen Z kids," Mrs. Usha laughed. "There's nothing they can't learn if they set their minds to it!"

"Really, Gauhar, your chicken and paneer curries are just delicious," Mrs. Fatima chimed in, her voice tinged with nostalgia. "They remind me of our hostel days. We used to look forward to your cooking so much!"

"I'm starting to worry about myself," Farah chuckled, a playful glint in her eye. "I hope my cooking classes pay off before my wedding bells ring this winter."

"Don't worry, beta!" Mrs. Usha reassured her with a lighthearted grin. "Times have changed. It's all about teamwork in the kitchen these days. I've already told Ravi he needs to learn a few kitchen skills before he gets married!"

The ladies burst into laughter, the air filled with camaraderie and the aroma of delicious food as they continued to savor the dishes spread out before them.

5

Mahin gently warmed the chapatis, feeling the stiffness as they softened slightly in her hands. The Chicken do Pyaaza was nearly gone, just a smear of masala left clinging to the bowl. A small portion of rice and paneer remained, barely enough for one person.

The Baigan ka Bharta, though, sat untouched, perfectly garnished in its serving bowl as if waiting for someone to notice it.

She quietly took three spoonfuls of it, eating it with the warmed chapatis, the flavors rich but tasting faintly of disappointment. She finished the last of the paneer with rice, scraping every bit from the bowl. Then she spotted the lone rasgulla sitting in its syrup, a rare sweetness she allowed herself to enjoy.

The guests had finally left, their laughter and chatter fading into the night. One by one, everyone retreated to their rooms, the house settling into a quiet calm. Farhan, after exchanging the last polite goodbyes with Adil at the door, made his way back to the dining room.

"Do you need any help?" Farhan asked as he watched Mahin clear the table, stacking plates with practiced ease.

"No, it's fine. I've got it," Mahin replied, her voice light but firm.

"Come on, let me at least help with the dishes," Farhan insisted, stepping closer, his hands itching to pitch in.

"Really, Farhan, it's all right. I can handle it," Mahin said, giving him a reassuring smile. "Just check on Abbu, will you? Make sure he's taken his medicine."

Farhan hesitated for a moment, then nodded. "Okay, but call me if you need anything."

"I will," Mahin promised, heading into the kitchen, her movements swift and efficient. Farhan watched her for a moment before returning to the lounge.

Mahin washed the dishes with steady hands, her mind wandering. She cleared away the scraps into the bin, but when she reached the bowl of untouched Baigan ka Bharta, she paused. With a gentle sigh, she wrapped it carefully and placed it in the fridge, her favorite dish left uneaten.

As she closed the fridge door, a soft chill lingered in the air, a quiet reminder of what was set aside, waiting to be noticed.

Ehsaas Isharon ke

1

"Khalid bhai, I've been watching you every day for the past six months," Prakhar said, unable to hold back his curiosity any longer.

"You're here, on this same spot, rain or shine, always right at 4 p.m. You stay until 7, sometimes even longer. Like last Saturday—you didn't leave until 9. You don't speak to anyone, and your eyes are always locked on something in the distance. It's like the world could end around you, and you wouldn't even notice. I can't help but wonder—what keeps you here, day after day?"

Khalid took a slow, deliberate drag from his cigarette, letting the smoke linger around him before he ground the butt into the dirt beneath his heel. He said nothing, just stared off into the distance with that same distant look in his eyes.

Before Prakhar could press him further, Riyaz bhai chimed in with a sly grin, "Prakhar bhai, aap bilkul fazool mein waqt barbaad kar rahe hain. Apne Khalid bhai toh purane ashiq hain, kuchh nahi bolenge!"

"Arey, Riyaz bhai, kuchh toh batao!" Prakhar pleaded, his curiosity piqued. "Kya hua tha? Koi ladki thi kya? Usne uska dil toda? Woh uski classmate thi ya junior?"

Riyaz bhai chuckled, leaning back as if savoring the moment. "Arey, ladki nahi, madam se pyaar ho gaya tha bhai ko. Aur yeh aaj bhi hai, aur kal bhi rahega," he added, his voice taking on the playful tone of Mohammad Rafi's iconic song from Khuda Bhi Aasmaan Se. The familiar melody hung in the air, and soon enough, everyone around burst into laughter.

But Prakhar wasn't laughing. He was surprised at how casually everyone seemed to treat the whole situation, as if it were some light-hearted joke. Meanwhile, Khalid didn't seem to notice the banter at all, his gaze fixed on something only he could see.

Prakhar's curiosity deepened, and he turned back to Riyaz bhai, desperate for answers. "Bhai, mujhe inki love story janni hai. Please bataiye."

Still humming the song, Riyaz bhai waved him off with a dismissive hand. "Bohot lambi story hai. Taha bhai yahin baithe hain, unse pooch lo. Hamein bahut kaam hai."

Prakhar's attention shifted to Taha, a dark-complexioned guy in his mid-twenties who was a familiar face at the canteen. Even though Taha had graduated a couple of years ago and moved on to a job as a management trainee, he still showed up at the canteen every now and then, often chatting quietly with Khalid.

"Taha bhai," Prakhar asked cautiously, "can you please tell me what happened to Khalid bhai? I've tried asking him many times, but he never says anything."

Taha took a slow drag from his cigarette, his eyes narrowing slightly as he studied Prakhar. He held his glass of tea in the other hand, the steam mingling with the smoke from his cigarette. His gaze was sharp, almost piercing, and it made Prakhar feel slightly uneasy, like he was being judged.

After what felt like an eternity, Taha finally spoke, his voice calm and measured. "Hmm, it's a long story," he said. "Not the first time someone's asked me to tell them, but I'll do it for you. You seem like a good guy. I like you. Sit down." He pulled up a stool and gestured for Prakhar to sit beside him.

2

Prakhar sat down, heart pounding with anticipation. He could sense that what he was about to hear wasn't just a story—it was a piece of someone's life, filled with emotions that ran deep and raw. As Taha took another drag from his cigarette, Prakhar leaned in closer, ready to listen.

"It was the first day of our final year when we first saw Amna ma'am. She was... really beautiful," Taha began, his voice filled with nostalgia.

"Bhai, woh nayi ma'am ko dekha kya?" Taha had exclaimed, practically bouncing on his feet.

"Nahin bhai, kaun hai?" Khalid replied, intrigued.

Taha led Khalid down the hallway to the first-year classroom where Amna ma'am was teaching her first class. They hid behind a pillar, peeking through the open door. There she was, writing on the board with an elegance that seemed almost unreal. She wore a graceful saree, her black heels clicked softly with each step, and her hair was neatly tied back. Golden bangles adorned her right wrist, clinking softly as she wrote, and her voice— gentle yet firm—filled the room with a quiet authority.

"She's going to be teaching us MIS and Supply Chain this year," Taha whispered with a grin. "It's going to be crazy!"

But Khalid wasn't listening. His eyes were locked on Amna ma'am, completely captivated. It was like everything else had faded away; he could barely hear Taha over the pounding of his own heart.

"Khalid! Are you listening?" Taha nudged him.

"Oh, yes, it will be great," Khalid muttered, but his mind was somewhere else entirely, still lost in that first sight of her.

A few weeks later, in the final-year classroom, Khalid sat at his desk, waiting with an unusual anticipation. When Amna ma'am finally entered, a hush fell over the room. She moved with the same grace, her presence commanding yet kind.

"Hello everyone," she began, her smile lighting up the room. "It's our first class, and I'd like to introduce myself. I'm Amna, and I'll be teaching you operations. We'll focus on discussion-based interactions with live projects, and I'm looking forward to active participation from all of you. So, feel free to reach out to me anytime."

As she spoke, Khalid felt a strange rush of emotions—an instant surge of oxytocin that made his heart thump louder. Every word she said seemed to resonate deep within him, like a melody he never wanted to stop hearing. Her presence was magnetic, and he was drawn to her in a way he couldn't explain. That day, he realized he wasn't just impressed by her; he was completely captivated, and he knew then that this feeling wasn't going away anytime soon.

"Bhai, tujhe lagta hai pyaar ho gaya hai," Taha said with a knowing grin, observing Khalid's behavior over the next few days.

"Khalid's routine had changed dramatically, and it was hard not to notice. He started arriving at college before anyone else. Initially, we used to commute together, and Khalid would pick me up on the way. But now, he'd head straight to college early, leaving me to arrive late. He'd set up the classroom meticulously, making sure everything was in place—the duster, markers, chalks, and projector. Sometimes, he'd even offer to carry Amna ma'am's bag. It was clear something was different, but you know how it is in a group of boys. When one of us develops a crush, it's a cause for celebration, and we treated Khalid's crush the same way.

During the fresher's event, while we were all busy performing and trying to impress the junior girls, there was Khalid, doing what we considered boring stuff. Instead of mingling with us, he was helping Amna ma'am organize the event, making sure everything was perfect and running smoothly. It was bittersweet to watch. On one hand, I was happy for him—he seemed to have found something that truly made him happy. But on the other hand, I was starting to worry about how he was distancing himself from us. And you know there's always a risk with such things, especially when it comes to these kinds of relationships. And, unfortunately, that risk became a reality for him."

"Riyaz bhai, ek round aur laga do," Taha called out, asking for another round of tea, as he continued his story.

"The strangest part was, Amna ma'am never questioned Khalid's closeness. She even responded to his late-night calls and sent him 'take care' and 'good night' messages. For a while, we actually thought Khalid might achieve the impossible. We started to believe he could win her over. So much so that we began sharing the song 'Malare' from the movie Premam and would often hum it when Amna ma'am was around. The song, as you might know, revolves around a romantic relationship between a student and his teacher. We didn't understand much of the Malayalam lyrics, but we could feel the emotion—the longing, the hope, the innocence of first love. It seemed fitting for Khalid's situation, even if it was just a dream."

There was a pause as Taha stared into his cup, lost in thought. The bittersweet memory of Khalid's innocent devotion and the naive hope that came with it hung heavily in the air."

"But that day changed everything for him," Taha began, his voice low and heavy with the weight of the memories. "I still remember it so vividly—Khalid walked into class, his usual calm self, when one of our classmates blindsided him with the news about Amna ma'am's marriage. The shock on his face, the way his whole demeanor shifted in an instant—it was like watching someone's whole world crumble right in front of you. After that, he disappeared. I didn't see him for days, and when I went to his house, he wouldn't even come to the door. He just shut himself away, completely withdrawing from everyone and everything."

Taha paused, taking a deep breath, as if trying to steady himself against the storm of emotions those memories stirred up. "I knew what he was going through," he continued, "but there was nothing I could do. Talking to Amna ma'am wasn't going to help. She was like a stone—devoid of any emotion. I kept wondering, if she didn't have feelings for Khalid, why did she let him get so close? Why did she encourage him? To me, it felt like she toyed with him, just like so many girls do. They keep you hanging in confusion, only to end up choosing someone more 'stable'—and that's exactly what happened with Amna ma'am. She went for the well-settled guy in the end."

Taha's voice cracked slightly as he went on, the frustration and helplessness clear. "It hurts even more because she wasn't just some young girl; she was his teacher. She should have known better. She should have acted with more responsibility. Look at Khalid now—he didn't even join the company he was placed with. He just stands there every single day, hoping to catch a glimpse of her, twice a day, like clockwork. That's his whole life now. Even when we drop by to chat, he's not really with us. His mind is always on her. I don't know what he's holding on to, or what he thinks his future could possibly look like, but he keeps it all to himself. Not once has he ever spoken her name or shared what's really in his heart."

Taha's eyes glistened with a mix of anger and sorrow as he continued. "And Amna ma'am? She just keeps walking past him, day after day, without a shred of guilt or shame. Sometimes, she even looks at him, but who knows what's going through her mind? It's like she doesn't care at all. Any decent person would have had the sense to change colleges or at least show some compassion. But not her. She's as hard as a rock, like she doesn't even have a heart. How can someone be so emotionless, so untouched by the pain they've caused?"

Taha's voice fell to a whisper, his words hanging in the air like a cloud of sadness. "I can't understand it. I don't think I ever will."

And then, as Taha's voice grew louder, cutting through the background hum of the open canteen, he suddenly erupted, "Iski zindagi se chali kyun nhn jati ye!"

In his outburst, Taha hurled his unfinished glass of tea against the nearby wall. The glass shattered on impact, sending shards flying, while the tea splattered across the white surface, leaving a dark, messy stain. The once clean and shiny wall was now marred by the mark of his frustration.

With a final, frustrated glance, Taha grabbed his bag and stormed out of the canteen. The sudden violence of the moment left everyone around stunned. Meanwhile, Khalid remained unmoved by the chaos, his gaze still fixed, lost in his own thoughts as if the commotion had never happened.

3

Amna addressed the first-year students with a tone of authority and encouragement. "Today, we discussed career advancement and planning in Management Sciences. It's crucial to be both ruthless and hardworking. In a world increasingly dominated by AI and GPT technologies, it's essential to continually upgrade your skills. I want to hear your thoughts on this. Don't hesitate to voice a differing opinion."

A hand shot up from the back of the room. "Ma'am, I beg to differ. Even though job competition is fierce, the human element can't be ignored!"

Amna turned her attention to Prakhar with a curious gaze. "Can you please elaborate, Prakhar?"

Prakhar stood up, his conviction evident. "Ma'am, organizations are created by humans for humans. We work as a team, caring for and supporting each other. If I don't feel like I belong to a company, I won't feel secure. I believe in taking everyone along with me, even if it means slowing my own progress. In the end, we need people we can trust and form bonds with, not just machines making decisions about our products."

A murmur of amused agreement spread through the classroom.

Amna nodded thoughtfully before responding. "Well, Prakhar, I appreciate your perspective. But let me put this into context with a question: "If you land an excellent placement after your master's, would you trade it for your best friend Neha?"

Neha's cheeks flushed, a mix of surprise and embarrassment washing over her. Amna's question had put her relationship with Prakhar in the spotlight.

Prakhar hesitated, then replied, "Ma'am, that's a hypothetical question, but I'll answer it. If Neha needed the job more than I did, I might consider giving it to her."

Amna smiled, her expression a mix of understanding and challenge. "See, Prakhar, that's where emotions can cloud judgment. Life isn't about making decisions on impulse. You need to be practical. To lead a better life and provide for others, you must first ensure your own financial stability. Sacrificing your career for others may seem noble, but it's often impractical. In the job market, those who perform are promoted, while those who only give may miss out on opportunities or face layoffs. That's the harsh reality."

Prakhar's face reflected deep thought. "But what if Neha means more to me than anything else? What if I truly believe her well-being is more important than my own career?"

Amna's eyes softened slightly. "Perhaps Neha would have a better answer to that. And she might find herself agreeing with me in a year or so."

Prakhar, now visibly emotional, asked, "Ma'am, what if someone actually sacrificed their career for you?"

Amna's face grew serious. "I'd consider that naive. Life doesn't work that way. That's just my belief."

As the class ended with no further questions, students began to pack up. Neha lingered, her mind racing with thoughts of Prakhar's willingness to sacrifice for her. A small smile played on her lips as she reflected on his devotion, even as the reality of Amna's words began to sink in.

4

"Amna ma'am, AMNA ma'am, it's me, Prakhar, your first-year student!"

Amna heard her name and turned to see Prakhar sprinting towards her, his face flushed and his breath coming in short, urgent gasps. His eyes were wide with a mix of excitement and desperation.

"We're done for the day, Prakhar," Amna replied, continuing to walk briskly. "No more questions. I'm already late for home."

"Ma'am, please, it's really important!"

"No, Prakhar, I have to go. See you tomorrow."

"It's about Khalid bhai!" Prakhar called out, his voice cutting through the air with urgency.

Amna stopped abruptly, her pace slowing. She took a deep breath and turned to face him, curiosity etched on her features. "What do you want to know?"

"I want to hear everything that's happened between you two. I know Khalid bhai's side, but I want to know yours."

"Oh, did he speak to you?" Amna asked, her tone shifting slightly.

"No, ma'am," Prakhar admitted. "But his friends did, and I've formed a very different opinion since then."

"Oh? What opinion?"

"That you're too emotionless. That you don't care for others. But I don't fully believe it. I think there's another side to the story."

"Hmm, it's complicated," Amna said with a hint of reluctance.

"Ma'am, please. It's a humble request. It's really important for me."

"Well, if you're thinking about Neha…"

"Not exactly, ma'am, but to some extent, yes."

"Honestly, you're not the only one with such opinions about me," Amna confessed. "I'm aware of what students say, especially the boys. But I'm glad you approached me. In fact, you're the first person to ask me directly."

"Ma'am, it won't take much time. Please, can you share your side of the story?"

Amna paused, then nodded. "Alright, but I won't drag it out."

She gestured for Prakhar to sit on a nearby bench along the pavement. As they settled, Amna took a moment to gather her thoughts, ready to reveal a part of her story that had long been shrouded in mystery.

"Khalid was my favorite. He always sat at the front, fully engaged, and often led the group discussions with an infectious energy. Sometimes, he even helped me understand the local customs and places. I recall a couple of times when he offered me a ride home to my PG. The first time was a bit awkward for me—I was standing outside the gate, waiting for a rickshaw, when Khalid stopped by and offered me a ride. Though he seemed confident in his words, I could sense his nervousness through his body language. When someone tries to act bold while feeling conscious, they tend to rush their speech and fidget a bit. For a moment, I thought about declining, but then I figured, what's the big deal? It's just a ride.

After that, there were numerous occasions where Khalid would offer me tea during college gatherings, bring me a chair when there was a shortage, clean the board and the desk before my arrival, and so on. It was an eventful year—more so now when I look back on it with the perspective I have today. I realize I took things for granted, not understanding how they were unfolding. Maybe it's because I never had such interactions before. In my own college days, I was a quiet, reserved student with few close friends. My friendships with male classmates were nearly nonexistent. We mostly stuck to our small group of girls, and talking to boys was something we only did on special occasions.

"Maybe that's why I couldn't gauge Khalid's feelings as they developed so rapidly, partly because I unintentionally encouraged all his attempts at communication. I didn't even see it as a friendship—it was just a normal interaction with another person. I was too ignorant, too unaware of what was brewing behind the scenes."

There was a sense of calmness in her voice as Prakhar tried to absorb what all was unfolding before him.

Amna's demeanor was pure, simple, and straightforward. She didn't shy away from sharing even her most personal memories.

Khalid, in contrast, was very reserved. Despite Prakhar's multiple attempts to get him to open up, he couldn't manage to get a single word from Khalid about his past.

A brief silence followed, during which Amna kept checking her watch. Before she could ask to leave, Prakhar came up with a new set of questions.

"So, when did Khalid first express his feelings openly? Did he propose to you?"

"Ah, not really," Amna replied, not particularly eager to keep the conversation going. She was already running a bit late and hadn't informed Jamal about this unexpected meeting.

Two years had passed since Amna and Jamal were married. Jamal worked as an SAP consultant at ASBES, a leading software development company, and his family's proposal had been an obvious choice for Amna and her parents. At thirty, he was well-established, with a promising career that seemed to stretch endlessly into the future. The match had come about thanks to Jamal's maternal uncle, Dr. Saud, a lecturer at Amna's college. He had watched her closely over the years and saw something in her—a quality he knew would complement his nephew.

He quietly initiated the introductions, and from there, everything moved quickly, as if it were meant to be.

Jamal was different from anyone Amna had ever known. Where she was reserved, he was open and expressive, forming a deep connection with her almost immediately. Every Friday evening, Jamal would pick her up from college, and they would retreat to the cozy corner of their favorite coffee shop in town. They would talk for hours, losing track of time, sharing dreams and stories over cups of steaming coffee. Jamal was clear-eyed about his goals and had a vision for their future that was both ambitious and reassuring. He knew exactly where he wanted to go and how he wanted to build their life together.

He also cared deeply about Amna's aspirations, always encouraging her to pursue her own path. Whether it was helping her prepare for a challenging presentation or offering guidance on difficult subjects like Management Information Systems and Supply Chain Management, Jamal was always there, his support unwavering. For Amna, Jamal was everything she had hoped for in a partner—thoughtful, kind, and endlessly patient. She often marveled at how fortunate she was to have found someone who understood her so completely and who brought such joy into her life. In Jamal, she had found not just a husband, but a true partner—a soulmate.

"Hey, did you hear? Amna ma'am is getting married!" Shazia exclaimed as all the students waited for class to start.

"Really? So many hearts will be broken! Booooo," cried Namrata dramatically.

"No, it can't be! What about me?" Faisal joked, pretending to be heartbroken before laughing to lighten the mood.

"Here comes Khalid—he must know the details. Our very own teacher radio jockey," Shazia exclaimed as Khalid entered the classroom.

"Khalid, what's the latest news? We're hearing all sorts of things!" Namrata asked eagerly.

"What news? I don't know what you're talking about," Khalid responded, looking genuinely surprised.

"As if you don't know! Haven't you been attending your evening lectures?" Tamanna chimed in, her voice dripping with sarcasm.

"Seriously, I have no idea what you guys are talking about. Can someone please explain?" Khalid replied, sounding a bit irritated by the unexpected questions from his classmates.

"Alright, let's make this simple for you," Shazia said bluntly. "The rumor is that Amna ma'am is getting married! But we have no clue who the lucky guy is, and we're dying to find out. So, care to fill us in, Khalid?"

There was a brief pause before Khalid, forcing a hesitant smile, replied, "Oh, that's great news. I didn't know about that. I'll let you know if I hear anything," and quickly left the classroom.

His footsteps slowed as he walked down the corridor, the weight of the conversation sinking in.

From now on, Khalid's life would change forever. He wouldn't wake up in the morning eager to check his phone for a late-night message from Amna ma'am. He wouldn't spend time deciding which shirt to wear to college, or carefully choosing his cologne, or making sure to shave every day for a clean, polished look. Those days were over.

There would be no more frantic rush to get to college on time, skipping breakfast and racing his bike through traffic just to arrive early. The days would stretch out endlessly, and the nights would become unbearable. No more tossing and turning in his bed; now, he would lie there in silence, staring up at the ceiling, his brow damp with sweat. His eyes would refuse to close. The white ceiling above him would become a screen, replaying memories of her on an endless loop.

Lost in thought, Khalid barely noticed he had reached the dead end of the corridor. He almost walked straight into the wall before his toes brushed against it. Shaking himself out of his daze, he looked up, turned right, and headed straight for Amna ma'am's office.

He paused outside her door, trying to clear his head. Then, taking a deep breath, he opened it. "Ma'am, may I come in?"

"Yes, Khalid, please do," Amna said, looking up from her desk.

"Khalid, could you help me organize these papers by serial number? I've been swamped with this pile of junk all morning," she asked, handing him a bundle of exam papers.

He took the papers without a word and pulled up a chair. He set his bag down beside him and quietly started sorting through the stack, occasionally glancing at Amna, who remained absorbed in her work.

After a few moments, he finally spoke up, his voice hesitant. "Ma'am, can I ask you something?"

"Of course, Khalid," she replied without looking up.

"Are you getting married?"

Amna looked up, surprised. "Oh, Khalid, I'm so sorry. I completely forgot to mention it to you. Everything happened so quickly. Yes, his name is Jamal. Let me show you a picture."

She started scrolling through her phone, then handed it to Khalid with a smile. "Here he is. Look."

Khalid stared at the photo of Amna and Jamal, smiling brightly in a selfie, each holding a cup of coffee.

"He looks nice. You both seem happy," Khalid said quietly, handing the phone back to her.

"Yes, I didn't expect it to happen so soon. I didn't even know him at first, but we connected right away. He's really wonderful. I'll introduce you two someday; I think you'd like him," Amna said warmly.

Khalid slumped back in his chair, taking a deep breath. He finished organizing the papers without another word and left the room quietly.

For the next two weeks, Khalid disappeared. No one saw him, and his phone was unreachable despite Taha, his best friend, trying to call him multiple times. When Taha and Rizwan visited Khalid's house, his mother told them he wasn't feeling well and didn't want to see anyone.

Amna noticed his absence too. He had missed ten classes in a row, something he had never done before. She tried messaging him, but her messages went unanswered. She even asked around, but his friends had no answers.

"You seem worried today. Is something bothering you?" Jamal asked one evening as they sat together.

"Yeah, one of my students, Khalid, hasn't been to class for several days. No word from him at all. We were working on a paper with a deadline coming up, but I haven't heard anything from him," Amna explained.

"Oh, don't stress about these boys. They're all like that at this age—unfocused and unsure about their careers. Let them get a taste of the real world for a few years," Jamal said dismissively.

"No, Khalid isn't like that. He's always been responsible. This is the first time he's ever done something like this, and I still have to draft a reply to the editor," Amna replied, a hint of concern in her voice.

"Hey, don't let this ruin our evening. I'm here to help if you need it, but try to relax while we're together," Jamal said, smiling.

"Hmm, you're right. Let's just order our coffee," Amna agreed, forcing a smile.

It was the 5th of November, and Amna was walking to college as usual. As she passed the college canteen, she saw Khalid standing there, hands in his pockets, watching her.

"Khalid! Where have you been? I've been trying to reach you so many times. Meet me in my office after class," she called out as she walked by, not waiting for his reply.

Khalid stood still, watching her disappear into the building, his expression unreadable.

"Khalid, I called you multiple times! Where have you been? I was waiting for you all evening," Amna demanded as she confronted him. He was standing in the same spot where she had seen him that morning. The campus was empty now, the canteen owner packing up for the night.

"Sorry, ma'am, I didn't mean to—" Khalid started, his voice barely above a whisper.

"What do you mean you didn't mean to? What's wrong with you? You're not answering your phone, not replying to messages, and now you're ignoring me when I ask to meet?" Amna's frustration was palpable.

"Sorry, ma'am, I'm just not feeling right," Khalid muttered.

"What happened? Is everything okay at home?" Amna asked, her tone softening slightly.

"No, ma'am, everything is fine."

"Then what is it? What's going on?"

"Nothing, ma'am," he mumbled again.

"Seriously, Khalid, you've never been like this before. We're running out of time on our deadline, and I've heard nothing from you!"

"Sorry, ma'am," he repeated, still not meeting her eyes.

"'Sorry'? Do you have any idea what I've been dealing with these past few days? My inbox is flooded with emails from the editors. If I don't send them the final draft, they might reject our paper entirely!" Amna's voice rose with urgency.

"Yes, ma'am," he said quietly.

"'Yes, ma'am'? Are you going to help me finish it or not?"

Khalid said nothing, his silence stretching painfully between them

"Khalid, I'm talking to you!" Amna pressed, her frustration mounting.

Still, there was no response.

"Khalid, do you hear me?" she asked again, her voice breaking a little.

But Khalid just stood there, head bowed, silent.

"Never mind," Amna said, turning away in exasperation.

"I love you, ma'am," Khalid blurted out, his voice trembling before he suddenly broke down into uncontrollable sobs. Tears streamed down his face, which had turned bright red. He was gasping for air between hiccups, his entire body shaking with the force of his emotion.

Amna froze. She didn't know what to say or do. She could only watch as Khalid wept, a young man who had always been so calm, responsible, and full of life now crumbling before her eyes. His shoulders sagged as if the weight of the world had crushed him.

She opened her mouth to speak but found no words. Helpless, she slowly turned away and started to walk, her steps unsteady. Her face had gone pale, and her body trembled with each step. Behind her, Khalid's sobs continued, his head still bowed, until the evening fog blurred him from her sight.

"I couldn't sleep that night. I didn't even answer Jamal's calls," Amna later recounted, her voice heavy with reflection. "How could I not have seen Khalid's feelings? I sat frozen in my room, replaying everything that had happened. I took a couple of days off to try and sort out my thoughts. I didn't even respond to the editor, and eventually, our paper got canceled. But at that moment, more was at stake than a paper. I couldn't figure out what was happening inside me. It wasn't that I was heartbroken or felt betrayed—I never loved Khalid like that. I genuinely liked him as a person. And I had no doubts about marrying Jamal. But Khalid's confession—it caught me off guard. It made it hard to think straight."

When I returned to college, I saw Khalid standing at the canteen again, watching me as I walked by. I looked at him but didn't say anything. He just stood there, waiting for me, day after day, and when I left in the evening, he would still be there, silent and unmoving, watching as I passed by. He never spoke a word.

Amna had lost track of time as she recounted her story, and Prakhar listened intently, his expression calm and thoughtful.

"One day, I decided to talk to him. I made sure everyone had left. Like every other day, Khalid was standing there, waiting for me. But when he saw me walking toward him, his eyes dropped, and he looked away."

"Khalid, I want to talk to you," Amna called out, her voice firm.

He didn't respond.

"Khalid!" she said again, more forcefully.

"Yes, ma'am," he replied, still staring at the ground.

"Look at me and talk to me," Amna insisted.

Slowly, Khalid raised his eyes to meet hers.

"Khalid," Amna began, her voice soft but filled with concern, "I know you're hurt, and I want you to know that I never intended to cause you any pain. I had no idea you felt this deeply. I genuinely enjoyed your company, but it was more in the context of our student-teacher relationship. I appreciated your gestures as signs of respect and care. I always believed in your sincerity and hard work. But I'm worried that these feelings might lead you down a path from which you may never return."

Amna paused, trying her best to offer comfort, though it was clear this was not her strong suit. "Khalid, are you listening?"

"Yes, ma'am," Khalid murmured, still staring at the ground.

"Come, sit down," Amna said gently, reaching out and guiding him to a nearby table. "Let's talk."

As they sat together, Amna continued, her voice tinged with sadness. "Khalid, I've already committed myself to someone I intend to spend my life with. You are incredibly important to me, but our relationship is fundamentally different. You can't force something that isn't meant to be, and the more you try, the more it will hurt you."

Khalid listened in silence, his eyes still fixed downward.

"It's best for you to focus on your final exams," Amna advised, her tone earnest. "You've secured a good placement, and I'm confident you have a bright future ahead. Standing here and waiting for me won't help; in fact, it will only prolong your suffering."

"Are you hearing what I'm saying?" Amna asked gently.

"Yes, ma'am," Khalid replied quietly.

"Listen, Khalid, I truly care about you," Amna said gently, her voice carrying a mix of concern and frustration. "I want to see you succeed, to achieve great things in life, to chase after what you really desire."

Khalid took a deep breath, and for the first time in days, he spoke, his voice low and steady. "Ma'am, I've never questioned your decision. I haven't argued or caused any trouble. I've respected your choice. Now, you need to respect mine."

Amna's brow furrowed as she tried to understand. "What choice, Khalid? Coming here every day just to catch a glimpse of me, a few moments at a time?"

"You won't understand, Ma'am," Khalid replied, his voice barely above a whisper.

"No, I won't," she shot back, her patience wearing thin. "And I don't want to." With that, she slammed her hand down on the table, turned sharply on her heel, and stormed out of the canteen, leaving a stunned silence in her wake.

"I think I need to call a cab," Amna muttered, trying to compose herself. Prakhar, still riveted by the unfolding story, pressed on.

"Ma'am, just one more thing," he asked quietly, hesitating. "I've seen you look at Khalid bhai when you walk by. Doesn't it stir any emotions in you?"

Amna paused, a heavy sigh escaping her lips. "Prakhar, life after marriage isn't like it's portrayed in movies or books. Emotions change, they evolve. You don't sing for your partner every day, or dance in the rain like some romantic fantasy. Real life is about daily struggles—work, commuting, dealing with in-laws. Love becomes something different. It's still there, but it's not the kind of love you dream about. Jamal and I love each other, but we barely get a moment to really talk, to share what we're feeling. Sometimes I crave a simple, comforting hug, but even that feels out of reach. I know there's a void in our lives, a gap between what we want and what we have."

She glanced down the road, lost in thought for a moment before continuing. "When I see Khalid, I see how much he yearns for me. It's like he wants nothing more than to make me happy, to brighten my day in any way he can. But he's living in a different world, a different reality. Our paths can never truly cross again, but somehow, our emotions do. He fills that void for me, even if just a little, and in return, I give him a smile when I can. It's the only kindness I can offer him, the only bit of light I can give to his day. I know people might judge me for it, but if it brings him even a tiny bit of happiness, then it's worth it. That's all I can give, given how emotionally inept I am. And that's that."

Just then, the cab pulled up to the curb. Amna gave Prakhar a final, distant look before stepping inside. As the car drove away, her figure faded into the dusk, swallowed by the gathering night.

Prakhar stood there for a moment, lost in thought, before heading back to the canteen. Khalid was gone. The shattered glass Taha had thrown the other day had been swept up by Riyaz bhai, but the stain on the wall remained, at least for now.

Old School

1

Bilal glanced over Sayyeda's presentation for the upcoming conference, tapping his fingers lightly on the edge of her study desk. She sat absorbed, finalizing the slides on her laptop, but his sharp gaze didn't miss the subtle flaws.

"I feel you need to cite references from top journals," Bilal said, breaking the silence, his voice steady yet firm. "Papers from predatory journals might not be appreciated in academia."

Sayyeda sighed, her fingers hovering above the keyboard, her thoughts drifting to Bilal. He had always been meticulous, almost obsessively so, about maintaining order and high standards in every aspect of his life. Their home office was a reflection of that — shelves neatly arranged with books, both academic and otherwise, in perfect symmetry. Fiction, non-fiction, historical accounts, scientific journals — each had its place, with not a single volume out of order. It was a haven of learning, but also a symbol of Bilal's relentless need for structure.

Even their son, Sahil, wasn't spared from this strict regimen. Bilal insisted he spend at least an hour each day reading, no matter the genre. And heaven forbid a book was left slightly askew — Bilal would notice immediately. The tiniest speck of dust on the shelves or a stray papers left in the wrong place would set him off. He had an almost compulsive need to maintain cleanliness and order, not just at home but everywhere. Walking down the street, he'd shake his head in frustration at the litter or comment on the lack of civic sense. At work, his fastidiousness extended to his colleagues, which often led to irritation.

Bilal's colleagues would dodge his gaze, aware that he was likely to point out something they hadn't done to his standards. Conversations with him felt like interrogations, and people found excuses to leave quickly. His team, in particular, grew weary of his strict rules — logging into meetings five minutes early, adhering to rigid deadlines, and sticking to his meticulously planned schedules. While Bilal thrived on this routine, it became a source of quiet resentment among those around him.

At home, his expectations were no different. He insisted on fixed times for meals, early mornings, and a structured day. Sayyeda, however, rarely adhered to these demands, which led to his constant, albeit futile, reminders. Over the years, she had grown increasingly resistant to his controlling nature, her silence in response to his lectures a kind of quiet rebellion. Yet, Bilal never seemed to notice her detachment. He continued to speak his mind, oblivious to how little of it was heard.

For Bilal, reading wasn't a pastime; it was a discipline. Every morning at four, he would settle in the library, poring over a book, immersing himself in pages while the rest of the world still slept. He had even tried to get

Sayyeda to follow the same routine, but her love for reading was sporadic at best. She had started a few novels, autobiographies even, at Bilal's suggestion, but could barely scrape through a few pages before her interest fizzled out.

What truly captured her attention, much to Bilal's dismay, were the evenings spent with Ammi in front of the television, watching endless episodes of Kaun Banega Crorepati or The Kapil Sharma Show. Bilal couldn't understand it, nor did he try to hide his disapproval.

"I suggest you look up top journals or authors in sustainable development," Bilal continued, oblivious to her drifting thoughts. "Maybe refer to the ABS or ABDC list?"

"I understand, Bilal," Sayyeda replied, exhaling quietly. She glanced at the books stacked neatly on Bilal's side of the desk, their imposing presence adding weight to his argument. "But there are so many papers published without citing the ones you're suggesting. Even my guide doesn't reference those journals. Most scholars in our field don't."

Bilal's brow furrowed, his irritation bubbling to the surface. "So you're saying mediocre work is acceptable?"

"Listen, Bilal," she shot back, frustration creeping into her voice. "You're not in the research field. You don't see what's happening today. Plenty of people publish without following these so-called elite lists."

"And that makes it right?" Bilal countered, his voice sharp now. "I may not be in academia, but I have a PhD. You know why I didn't pursue it further — there wasn't enough practical relevance in what I was doing. That doesn't mean I'm out of touch. I read journal articles, I keep myself updated."

Sayyeda turned her chair to face him fully, eyes flashing. "Then immerse yourself in it if you care so much! Do you even know what we deal with every day? Journals are controlled by cartels. If you don't have the right networks, you're not getting published. And those thousands of citations you see? It's all a scam."

Bilal crossed his arms, unyielding. "So what, because the system's broken, you should just give up and follow the herd? I stepped away to contribute to society in a real, tangible way, not to chase academic points."

"Tell that to the university professors who only care about API scores," she muttered, half under her breath.

"That's because you haven't been exposed to what people are doing globally." His tone softened, but the edge remained. "Take your work, for instance. If you had referred to quality journals, you'd have a better understanding of where your research fits in the bigger picture."

"And what's so wrong with my work, then?" she challenged.

"Look at your model for sustainable waste management in India," Bilal began. "You've suggested awareness drives, educating rural populations, incentivizing NGOs — but there's nothing concrete. You mentioned pitching your ideas to Professor Mike, but if you'd reviewed his work, you'd see how he grounds his strategies in real interventions. Just the other day, I was reading about his work with housemaids in Kolkata. He's developing solutions to reduce waste in households where working women don't have time to manage kitchens."

Bilal paused for a moment, trying to gauge if Sayyeda was following, then pressed on.

"In Kolkata, Mike noticed that working women, especially those from middle-class families, often struggle to find time to manage their kitchens. They rely heavily on housemaids for cooking and cleaning. But here's where the problem arises. The maids, often untrained in sustainable practices, end up wasting a significant amount of food, water, and other resources during meal preparation and cleanup. For instance, they dispose of leftover food instead of reusing or storing it, or they leave taps running while washing dishes, leading to water wastage."

Bilal's voice quickened, the words coming more fluidly as he delved into the specifics of the research. "Mike didn't just observe these issues; he developed a concrete intervention program. He started by training the maids on sustainable practices, teaching them simple but effective ways to reduce waste. This included everything from optimizing the use of water and reusing leftovers, to planning meals in ways that minimize excess. His approach wasn't just theoretical — he tested it in several households across Kolkata."

"He even conducted workshops where both the employers — the working women — and their maids participated. The workshops helped bridge the gap between the two groups, ensuring that both parties were aligned on waste management goals. Mike's research didn't stop at education; he followed up by monitoring the impact over several months. The results were significant. Households that implemented his strategies saw a measurable reduction in food and water waste, and even in energy consumption."

Bilal leaned back slightly, his gaze steady on Sayyeda. "The most interesting part, though, is that Mike's research is now expanding. He's looking to replicate these interventions in other regions of India, tailoring the approach to local conditions. He's particularly interested in collaborating with researchers who can help him understand how these solutions can be adapted for rural areas or different cultural contexts."

Bilal's enthusiasm was unmistakable. "This is where you come in. You're working on sustainable waste management, right? Imagine how much more powerful your work could be if you incorporated real interventions like this. You could study how such training could be applied in different settings, maybe even in rural areas where waste management issues are different but just as pressing."

Sayyeda, who had been quietly listening, her expression shifting from frustration to contemplation, finally spoke. "But Bilal, that's so far removed from my current focus. I'm looking at broader models, not just specific cases like housemaids and kitchens."

"I get that," Bilal replied, his voice softening. "But that's exactly my point. Theoretical models are important, but connecting them to practical, on-the-ground work gives them relevance. Look at Mike's research — it's not just about writing papers. He's actively solving a problem, and his findings are being applied in real households. That's the kind of impact you could have."

He leaned forward again, a hint of urgency in his voice. "I'm not saying abandon your theoretical work. Just think about complementing it with something like this. Mike is actively seeking collaborators, and you're going to Stockholm soon. Why not reach out to him, propose an idea that builds on his work? Interview some households before you go, gather data on the challenges working women face in managing waste. It doesn't have to be big, but it could add a practical dimension to your work that the conference committee would really appreciate."

Sayyeda threw up her hands, exasperated. "It's too much, Bilal! I can't keep up with all these practical solutions you keep throwing at me. I have enough on my plate without chasing after Professor Mike. Theoretical work will be appreciated more than this hands-on stuff you keep suggesting."

"I'm not against theory," Bilal said, his voice steady again. "But it should solve real problems. Even Einstein's theory of relativity had practical applications. Satellites wouldn't work without his insights."

"Bilal," she interrupted, her voice breaking slightly. "I won't be able to make you understand. I have too much to deal with — Ammi's health, Sahil's school, and Laiba still being on milk. I'm juggling everything while you stay engrossed in your own world. You don't even know when Sahil's tests are or when Laiba needs soothing. You just show up when dinner is served. And now, you expect me to meet your academic standards? Let me go to the conference in peace, without adding to my burden."

Before Bilal could respond, Sayyeda stood up abruptly, leaving the room to arrange dinner.

2

"Ammi, have you taken your BP medicine?" Sayyeda asked, her voice soft yet edged with concern, as she spooned some palak paneer onto her plate. The aroma of freshly ground spices filled the dining room, momentarily masking the undercurrent of tension still lingering from her earlier conversation with Bilal.

Ammi looked up from her plate, blinking as if the question had pulled her from a distant thought. "Oh, I forgot, beta," she said with a slight wince. "Sahil, beta, can you bring my pouch from the dressing table?" She turned to her grandson, who sat beside Bilal, diligently scooping up mashed potatoes with sauce.

Bilal, seated across from Sayyeda, had already served himself a generous portion of paneer and chapatis. He was a man who ate with intention, savoring each bite in a way that rarely needed words. Even in the midst of their disagreements, food had always been a common ground between them. Bilal was a lover of home-cooked meals, and though he seldom vocalized his appreciation, the way he relished every bite was all the validation Sayyeda needed.

Sayyeda had learned early in their marriage that the kitchen was not just a place to cook but a bridge between them. Ammi had often reminded her, even before she became Bilal's wife, that food could be a balm for even the most troubled hearts. "A successful relationship always revolves around the kitchen," Ammi used to say, her voice carrying the weight of experience. "Your father and I had our disagreements, but once the food was served, we left everything behind."

"Ammi, how many times have I told you? Why do you keep forgetting?" Sayyeda's voice broke the comfortable hum of the dinner table, her tone a mix of concern and frustration. Her fork hovered above her plate, the palak paneer she had just served herself now forgotten.

"I'm really sorry, beta. I try to remember, I really do. But sometimes…" Ammi's voice trailed off, her frail hands fiddling with the edge of her dupatta, a familiar gesture of discomfort.

"That's not a good enough answer, Ammi," Sayyeda said, her voice sharpening. "You need to remember. Maybe set some reminders, or ask Sahil to help. The doctor was very clear — we have to be careful with your doses."

Bilal, who had been quietly engrossed in his meal, finally lifted his gaze from his plate, the rhythmic clinking of his fork against the porcelain pausing. Without looking up fully, he interjected, still chewing the last bite of his chapati. "It's going to keep happening unless she starts documenting everything. Medications, doses, times—it should all be written down."

He took a slow sip of water, the glass resting momentarily on his lips before he placed it back on the table with a measured clink. Now he looked at both women, his voice matter-of-fact. "Everything should be documented properly. That's how you avoid mistakes."

"How is that even possible, Bilal? Please be practical," Sayyeda shot back, the edge in her voice growing sharper.

"Why not?" he replied, his tone calm but steely. "I do it. I maintain a diary. I chalk out my schedule every night before bed. I know every appointment, every plan, down to the last detail, so I don't miss anything important."

"And do you allot time in your precious schedule to spend with Sahil and Laiba?" Sayyeda's frustration bubbled to the surface now, her eyes narrowing. "Or maybe a few minutes to have a casual conversation with us? Because, honestly, Bilal, your strict routine seems to revolve only around your work and your books. You've become like a machine. And we—your family—we're not machines. We can't live like that."

"Tell me, when was the last time you checked Sahil's schoolwork? Or sang Laiba to sleep? Or even asked Ammi if she's taken her meds on time?" Her voice rose, matching the tension in the room.

"How does that relate to this?" Bilal's frustration flared, his voice now a touch louder. "Why do you always drag these things into every conversation?"

"I manage so many other things," he continued, his tone defensive. "Banks, fees, bills, mortgages, all of it. I take care of those responsibilities so you don't have to worry."

"That's the problem, Bilal. You think everything can be neatly divided into 'your responsibility' and 'my responsibility.' But life doesn't work like that. You can't just shut off from everything that's happening around you and expect us to be perfect in our roles." Her voice trembled slightly, the weight of her words hanging heavy between them.

Ammi, who had been quietly eating, looked up, her eyes darting between her son and daughter-in-law, her hands now nervously clutching the edges of her plate. "Oho, please," she said softly, her voice pleading. "Calm down, both of you. Have dinner in peace."

But neither seemed to hear her.

Bilal's face hardened, his eyes locking onto Sayyeda's with a sharpness that made the air in the room feel heavy. "So what are you suggesting?" he asked, his voice low but simmering with anger. "Should I just forget about my work, start doing the dishes, play with the children all day, and sit around watching those useless soap operas with you and your mother?"

"You're impossible, Bilal!" Sayyeda's voice cracked with exasperation. "Just leave it. I don't have the energy for this. I have too much on my plate already. The conference is coming up, and I need peace — not this constant pressure." Her eyes were glistening now, her voice tight with the strain of it all.

"That's not a solution!" Bilal shot back, his frustration boiling over. "You can't just walk away every time we argue. You have to justify yourself—"

But before he could finish, the sound of Sayyeda's hands slamming against the table cut through his words. The force of it sent her plate rattling, the clatter of silverware breaking the conversation. Her eyes, wide and filled with a mix of anger and exhaustion, glared at him. "I've had enough, Bilal!" she yelled, her voice cracking under the weight of everything she had been holding in.

Without another word, she pushed her chair back, the screech of wood against the floor echoing through the dining room as she stormed out.

3

"Have you checked your ticket and passport?" Bilal's voice pierced through the morning air, the sharpness of his inquiry almost palpable, laced with an investigative tone that always grated on Sayyeda's nerves. It wasn't the question itself that irked her, but the manner in which it was posed—a cold, procedural checklist rather than a warm, caring farewell. She longed for a gentler parting, a hug perhaps, a tender reminder to stay safe, maybe even a simple promise: "I'll miss you. Call me when you land." But Bilal was not the sort to get lost in sentiment. His mind functioned like a clockwork machine—precise, practical, focused on logistics, leaving little room for emotions to clutter the gears.

He was the kind of man who, when faced with the richness of an experience, would see only the moving parts: the packing list, the itinerary, the checklist of belongings. Where others might dream of the places they would visit, the beautiful sunsets, the stories they would bring back, Bilal would hone in on the practicality of the trip—did she have enough cash? Was the schedule efficient? Were meetings properly arranged? He had always been this way, critical of any plan that veered too much towards the frivolous, towards that which he thought inconsequential. For him, life was a series of tasks to be completed with precision.

"Yes, I have everything in place. You don't need to worry," she replied, her voice laced with a faint sting of irritation that she couldn't quite hide. It wasn't that she didn't appreciate his concern, but there was no warmth in his words—just another lecture, another set of instructions as if she were a student who needed constant supervision.

"Good," he nodded, his gaze briefly flickering from his phone. "Make sure you double-check everything after the immigration check. And avoid eating anything heavy before the flight; it could make you uncomfortable." His words fell between them like stones—dense, devoid of tenderness, sounding more like a command than advice borne from love.

"Okay," she muttered, pulling the handle of her small stroller as she turned toward the departure gates, a half-hearted attempt at a smile disappearing as quickly as it came. "Bye."

She walked away, her steps steady but her heart heavy. As she neared the entrance, she paused, turning back for one final glance. Through the glass panes of the airport entryway, she raised her hand, waiting, hoping to catch his eye one last time. But Bilal was already deep in conversation, his phone glued to his ear, immersed in a world that had no space for goodbyes. He began to walk toward the parking lot, paused for a moment as if sensing her gaze, and then—without turning around—carried on.

Sayyeda stood there, her hand still raised, the weight of unspoken words heavy in the air between them. She sighed, lowering her hand slowly, her heart aching with a familiar disappointment. How many times had she imagined a different parting? A kiss, a simple wave, even a gesture—a small heart-shaped sign made with his palms. Something, anything. But Bilal had always been like this, practical to the point of being distant, his emotions buried beneath layers of responsibility and reason.

She lingered in that moment, feeling the loss of something that had never fully blossomed between them. Ten years of marriage, and still, she yearned for a warmth that he seemed incapable of giving. It wasn't that he didn't love her—she knew, deep down, that he did. But somewhere along the way, in the ebb and flow of life's demands, the small gestures of affection had slipped through the cracks.

People grow old not in years, but in the spirit, she thought. They become too practical, too cautious, their once-lively souls fading like the memories they've forgotten to cherish.

Bilal hadn't always been this way. She remembered a time before the routines had swallowed them whole— when they were still engaged, when he would make time for a coffee date, or even a movie night. She smiled faintly at the memory of their trips to the cinema. Bilal, ever the critic, would dissect the films with a clinical precision— debating the plot holes, the actors' performances, the creeping rot of nepotism in the industry. But at least then, they had shared something—a night out, a moment away from the world. They laughed, argued, and talked.

But that was before Sahil. Before Laiba. Before his promotion to senior manager had filled their lives with an endless stream of meetings, deadlines, and obligations.

Now, even when they were together, Bilal's mind was elsewhere—focused on what the kids should eat, how many calories were in each dish, whether the food was too fatty. Their drives together had turned into one-sided lectures about the state of the world, Bilal's voice a constant stream of criticisms: the bad driving, the broken systems, the failures of the administration. He would complain about how the authorities were more interested in making money than fixing problems, railing against the world with a passion that had once been reserved for her.

Sayyeda shifted the weight of her bag, glancing at the airport's timetable. Her flight, a two-hour journey to somewhere far from this heavy reality, was flashing on the screen. She stepped forward into the check-in line, the disappointment she carried with her heavier than the baggage the airline allowed.

As she handed over her passport and ticket, she couldn't help but wonder: was this how it was always going to be? Would they continue on this path—growing older, growing apart, their love buried beneath the weight of the mundane? Would she forever be the one waiting for a wave that never came, hoping for a gesture that remained locked in the recesses of his practicality?

The boarding pass in her hand felt cold, a ticket to somewhere that wouldn't be an escape, just a brief reprieve from the reality she would inevitably return to. And as she moved through security, one thought lingered in her mind: Was it enough to simply be loved in silence, or did she deserve more?

She exhaled softly, her steps blending into the faceless crowd of travelers, leaving behind the echoes of her unspoken goodbyes.

4

As Sayyeda waited for her turn to speak, her phone buzzed with a message from Bilal.

"Try to wrap up your presentation in under 10 minutes. Don't forget the cue cards. Take a deep breath before you start, keep your hands in front, elbows at 90 degrees. And remember to recite the dua."

She glanced at the message but didn't respond, slipping her phone back into her bag and turning her focus to the current presenter. Though she'd rehearsed her presentation countless times, standing in front of a room full of seasoned academics sent a nervous flutter through her. Her heart raced as her name was finally called.

Stepping to the dais, she took a steadying breath and began. "My research focuses on the importance of awareness programs in driving behavioral change," she began. "I developed a theoretical model that emphasizes how targeted educational campaigns and community engagement can shift household behaviors towards more responsible waste disposal."

She continued, "One of my key hypotheses is that consistent educational efforts, when combined with incentives for NGOs, can lead to significant improvements in waste management practices. For example, in the regions where these programs were implemented, we observed a measurable impact. Waste segregation practices improved by up to 40% in areas where these initiatives ran for over six months."

Her tone grew more confident as she shared her insights. "This data highlights how awareness, when strategically applied, can directly influence the way communities manage their waste, particularly in rural and underserved areas."

Professor Mike, the chair of the Sustainability track, leaned forward, tapping his pen lightly on the table. "Interesting work, Sayyeda. However, I'd like to hear more about how your findings could be implemented practically. You've presented a strong theoretical framework, but how do you see these insights being applied outside of academic contexts?"

Sayyeda hesitated for a moment but kept her composure. "Professor," she began, "my research focuses on the theoretical model of awareness-driven behavioral change, particularly in rural communities. For instance, one of my core hypotheses was that consistent educational campaigns would lead to improved household waste sorting, and our data supported this. In locations where these initiatives were run for over six months, waste segregation practices improved by 40%."

Professor Mike nodded but pressed further. "That's valuable, but the real challenge is translating those theoretical findings into everyday practices. How would you modify these programs to adapt to the varied conditions of actual communities, where the dynamics are more complex?"

There was a moment of silence as Sayyeda processed Professor Mike's question. Her mind raced, grappling with the challenge he had presented. She glanced briefly at her slides, taking in the carefully crafted visuals and data that had taken her weeks to compile. As she absorbed the weight of his inquiry, she could feel her heart pounding, the pressure of the moment amplifying her nerves.

"One approach could be to focus specifically on domestic helps, Professor. They're crucial in managing household waste, yet often overlooked in policy discussions. If we designed awareness programs specifically for them, we might see a more direct impact on household waste practices, especially in urban areas where they manage much of the kitchen waste."

Professor Mike's expression shifted, his interest visibly piqued. "Now that's an angle worth exploring. Targeting domestic helps could indeed provide a practical solution, particularly in developing countries where informal labor plays such a large role in daily life. I suggest you look into this in your future work."

"Thank you, Professor. I'll definitely explore that in the next phase of my research," Sayyeda said, feeling a wave of relief wash over her.

As she returned to her seat, her earlier tension melted away, replaced by quiet confidence.

She opened her WhatsApp to reply to Bilal about how her presentation had gone, but hesitated.

A whirlwind of emotions engulfed her. Frustration surged within her at Bilal's inability to grasp her feelings, compounded by the heaviness of his relentless lectures that often left her feeling diminished. Her pride, once steadfast, now wavered as she contemplated the potential influence of Bilal's research suggestions on Professor Mike. It felt as if every ounce of her confidence was being scrutinized under a magnifying glass, leaving her both vulnerable and introspective.

She put the phone down, feeling a sense of unease creeping in.

With a determined stride, she moved toward the gathering of delegates, ready to engage in conversation and network amidst the celebratory atmosphere of the Gala Dinner.

5

Sayyeda's replies to Bilal's incessant questions were brief, barely scratching the surface of her thoughts. Each message felt like an obligation rather than a conversation.

"Did you meet Prof. Mike?"

"Are you planning to visit the Stockholm Public Library?"

"What updates do you have from your meeting with the researchers at the Stockholm Environmental Institute?"

"Don't forget to check out the Swedish History Museum; it opens at 11 a.m. Swedish time. Try to make it on Sunday, as it will be closed on Monday."

"Do remember to review the checklist before you leave for India. I'll send you the same on your WhatsApp."

"Okay."

"I will."

"Got it."

"   "

With each response, she felt her irritation simmer just below the surface, but she didn't allow it to bubble over. Instead, she took her time exploring the vibrant marketplaces of Stockholm, including Svenskt Tenn, Handkraft Swea, and Hilda Hilda. She wanted to bring back something for everyone in her family, even the maid who cared for Laiba and their driver, Mufeed bhai, and his children—an act that she knew Bilal would not fully appreciate.

"Gifts? Seriously, I don't get it," Bilal would comment whenever she browsed for items to buy. "Try to get something useful. Either something related to learning or daily-use accessories. Spend your money wisely; you don't earn it that easily."

But in Stockholm, Sayyeda relished her independence, free from Bilal's critiques and lectures. Here, she felt a sense of peace wash over her, a quiet assurance that she could make her own decisions without scrutiny.

Freedom didn't mean being unaccountable; it meant having the right to make her own choices. Life was not simply a series of absolutes; it was a spectrum of perspectives. Whether it was the food she enjoyed, the content she consumed, or the hobbies she pursued, Sayyeda understood that one person's preferences could not dictate another's happiness. Everyone had the right to live life on their own terms.

With this newfound autonomy, she picked out a sipper and cute frocks for Laiba, a handheld game console for Sahil, a medicine box and a cozy sweater for Ammi, a scarf for the maid, and delectable chocolates for Mufeed bhai—she was certain his children would love them. As she meandered through the store, she paused in front of a display of men's perfumes. Aqua Di Gio from Armani caught her eye, its scent intoxicating and fresh. She loved it, even though Bilal always opted for Oud Itr, disapproving of the alcoholic content in most perfumes. She held the bottle up to her nose, savoring the aroma before reluctantly placing it back on the shelf.

Instead, she selected a plain blue shirt from Erla of Sweden, imagining how it would complement the grey pants Bilal often wore.

After a long, exhausting day, she retreated to her hotel, ordered dinner, and settled in to watch The Kapil Sharma Show. She scrolled through the photos she had taken during her travels, relishing the memories, and by 11 p.m., she fell asleep, content and ready for her early flight the next morning.

The plane touched down at Indira Gandhi International Airport at 5 p.m., and by 7 p.m., Sayyeda stood at the gate, scanning the crowd for Bilal. Instead, she spotted Mufeed bhai waving enthusiastically as he approached her with a warm smile, ready to assist with her luggage.

"Where is Bilal, Mufeed bhai? Is he waiting in the car?" she asked, her voice laced with anticipation.

"Ma'am," he said, his expression turning serious, "he asked me to receive you at the airport. We need to go directly to the hospital. Ammi's been admitted."

The news struck her like a bolt of lightning, cutting through the warmth of her homecoming.

6

Bilal sat slumped on the rusted bench just outside the hospital room, his head resting against the rough surface of a stained pillar. The metal frame of the bench, slightly bent from years of use, bore the weight of countless sleepless nights. His fingers, calloused and firm, were tightly clasped around a small, worn diary—a diary that had become his lifeline in this endless sea of uncertainty.

His face, softened in the depths of exhausted slumber, reflected the toll of countless days spent in worry and silent resolve. Beneath the bench, an unnoticed dark stain of pan spit marred the base of the wall, the kind of detail that would usually bother him—but not today. His chest rose and fell slowly, his breathing heavy, almost in sync with the rhythmic beeping of the machines behind the door.

Inside, Sayyeda stood at the narrow glass window of her mother's hospital room, gazing through the sterile partition at the fragile figure lying motionless on the bed. Ammi's chest rose and fell with the slow cadence of sleep, each breath monitored by the quiet hum of medical equipment. The screen beside the bed flickered softly, displaying a series of vital signs—pulse: 74, blood pressure: 81/125, oxygen saturation: 95%. The numbers were a fragile comfort, indicators of a delicate stability that could shift at any moment.

She opened the door carefully, the faint creak of the hinges loud in the otherwise muted room. The smell of antiseptic filled her lungs, and she instinctively took in the surroundings: the bed towering around her mother's frail frame, the sheets tucked in tightly by the nurses, the sterile air that seemed to hold its breath. Ammi's right hand, thin and marked by age, rested limply by her side, an IV drip inserted delicately into her wrist. Her face was peaceful, but the lines of time and pain etched deep into her skin betrayed the battle her body was enduring.

On the bedside table, a meticulous arrangement of papers caught her eye. She didn't need to guess who had organized them—Bilal, in his usual way, had left no detail unattended. She picked up the small stack, her fingers brushing against the first page of her husband's careful notes, the crispness of the paper contrasting with the emotional weight of what it contained.

Medications for Stroke Recovery:

Clopidogrel 75mg (Antiplatelet)

Dosage: One tablet in the morning, after breakfast.

Purpose: Prevents blood clots from forming and helps reduce the risk of another stroke.

Last Administered: 8:00 AM today.

Next Dose: 8:00 AM tomorrow.

Atorvastatin 40mg (Statin)

Dosage: One tablet at bedtime, after dinner.

Purpose: Lowers cholesterol levels and reduces the risk of heart complications post-stroke.

Last Administered: 9:00 PM yesterday.

Next Dose: 9:00 PM tonight.

Pantoprazole 40mg (Proton Pump Inhibitor)

Dosage: One tablet in the morning, before breakfast.

Purpose: Protects the stomach lining from potential damage caused by medications.

Last Administered: 7:30 AM today.

Next Dose: 7:30 AM tomorrow.

Levetiracetam 500mg (Anti-Seizure)

Dosage: Twice a day—morning and evening.

Purpose: Prevents seizures, common in stroke patients.

Last Administered: 8:30 AM today.

Next Dose: 8:30 PM tonight.

Blood Pressure Monitoring:

Target: 120/80 mmHg

Check frequency: 4-hour intervals.

Next check: 6:00 PM.

Daily Massage Routine for Stroke Recovery:

Foot Massage – Completed

Duration: 10 minutes, focused on increasing circulation.

Technique: Light strokes from heel to toes, circular motions on the ball of the foot.

Hand Massage – Completed

Duration: 10 minutes.

Technique: Gentle pressure on palm, stretching fingers individually to improve blood flow and flexibility.

Leg Elevation – Scheduled for 6:00 PM

Elevate the legs for 15 minutes to reduce swelling and improve venous return.

Ensure pillows are placed correctly under the knees and ankles for support.

Physiotherapy Exercises:

Wrist Twisting – 5 reps, twice daily

Instructions: Slowly rotate the wrist in a circular motion, clockwise and counterclockwise, holding for 5 seconds at each angle.

Finger Flexion and Extension – 10 reps, twice daily

Instructions: Open and close the hand slowly, spreading fingers wide and then curling them into a loose fist.

Neck Stretch – 3 reps, morning and evening

Instructions: Gently tilt the head to the left and right, holding for 10 seconds on each side.

Arm Raises – 5 reps, once in the morning and once in the evening

Instructions: Gently lift the affected arm above the head with assistance if needed, holding for 3 seconds at the highest point.

Leg Raises – 10 reps, twice daily

Instructions: Lying flat, raise one leg slowly, keeping it straight, hold for 5 seconds, then lower gently.

Doctors' Contacts:

Dr. Raghav Patel, Neurologist – +91 9876543210

Consultation: Stroke management, cognitive recovery.

Next meeting: Tomorrow at 10:00 AM for a progress review.

Dr. Anjali Mehta, Cardiologist – +91 9876543211

Consultation: Heart function post-stroke, cholesterol control.

Next meeting: Scheduled for Wednesday, 3:00 PM.

Nurses Assigned:

Nurse Priya – +91 9876543212

Shift: 7:00 AM to 3:00 PM.

Nurse Lakshmi – +91 9876543213

Shift: 3:00 PM to 11:00 PM.

Nurse Seema – +91 9876543214

Shift: 11:00 PM to 7:00 AM.

With a sigh, she quietly stepped out of the room. Her eyes immediately caught sight of Bilal's diary lying on the floor, having slipped from his tired grasp. His hands, once clutching it protectively, now rested open, palms upward as if in surrender. She bent down, carefully picking it up, her fingers brushing against the familiar worn leather cover. Opening it, her eyes fell on today's entry.

Today:

Ammi:

Ammi's pulse is steady today—74 bpm, BP holding at 81/125. Her oxygen level is stable at 95%. The doctors seem optimistic, but I can't take anything for granted. Her speech is still slurred, but she's trying. The physiotherapist mentioned slight improvements in muscle control during hand raises. I need to stay positive, keep motivating her, remind her that she's strong enough to fight this.

Her spirit is what will keep her going. I've set the alarm for Kaun Banega Crorepati tonight at 9 PM. It always brings a smile to her face. I'll ask Nurse Lakshmi to adjust her pillow so she can sit up to watch. I must remember to get her favorite biscuits from the canteen tomorrow—she hardly eats these days, but maybe those will entice her.

I worry about how she feels when she wakes up and doesn't see me. I've been trying to stay by her side as much as possible, but with everything piling up, I can't help but feel guilty when I step out for even a moment. I know she'd tell me to take care of myself, but I can't relax—not when she's lying there like that.

Sayyeda's Conference:

I haven't had time to follow up on her presentation for the Sustainable Urban Development conference. I know she's been working hard on it—especially with her collaboration with Prof. Mike. It's important for her planned project on Sustainable Waste Management in Developing Cities. I hope she properly attends all her sessions without worrying about Ammi. She has to focus on the paper, the discussions, and her networking opportunities. This project is too big to let distractions pull her away now.

Sent a message earlier with reminders for her return trip. Must check in with her tomorrow morning, make sure she has everything in place before she boards the plane.

Reminder List for Sayyeda:

Passport – Make sure it's in the front pocket of her sling bag, easily accessible for security.

Ticket – Double-check her return ticket from Stockholm to Delhi. Remind her to print a copy just in case.

Visiting cards – She's collected so many during this conference. Remind her to organize them so she doesn't lose any important contacts. Suggest she note key points on the back of each card for follow-up later.

Cash – She'll need some Euros for the airport, but also keep her Indian currency handy for when she lands back home. Make sure she has change for the cab ride from the airport.

Medicines:

Dimenhydrinate – The anti-nausea medication she sometimes forgets to take during long flights. Remind her to keep it in her handbag.

Her iron supplements—flight fatigue will hit her hard if she doesn't keep up with her dosage.

Soap papers & hand sanitizer – She's flying internationally, and hygiene is important. Remind her to keep these in her carry-on for easy access.

Napkins & tissues – In case of any spills or discomfort. She tends to overlook these small essentials but always needs them.

Notebook & pen – Her conference notebook must be packed, along with a backup pen for any last-minute notes or ideas.

Chargers – Laptop and phone chargers should be packed in her hand luggage, not the check-in bags. Also remind her about her power bank.

Presentation file – Ensure the final version of her presentation on Sustainable Waste Management is saved on her USB drive and her cloud storage, just in case.

Pending Tasks:

- Will text this reminder list to her later tonight. She might still be jet-lagged, so better to send it before she gets too busy with her final meetings in Sweden.
- Remind her to get some rest before the flight. The trip will be long, and she'll need her energy once she's back.
- Ask her how the meeting with Prof. Mike went. His feedback on the project could be critical for the next phase of research.
- Follow up on whether she's gotten the brochures and research materials she mentioned wanting to collect. She'll need those for the collaboration with Mike and her project with the university.

Family Management:

Sahil's School:

- Call Mrs. Iyer tomorrow to confirm Sahil's upcoming Mahatma Gandhi project. He'll need all the materials by the weekend. Remind him to start practicing his speech—it's important he doesn't wait until the last minute.
- Order the art supplies for Sahil (colored paper, markers, glitter) by tomorrow evening. Confirm with the maid that they'll arrive.
- Sahil has swimming lessons this week. Need to arrange transport for him if I can't get away from the hospital.

Laiba's Care:

- Remind the maid about Laiba's afternoon nap time—she's been skipping it lately, and it throws her whole routine off.
- Double-check Laiba's vaccination schedule. I think Dr. Nandini said her next shot is due on Monday, but I need to confirm the exact timing.
- Make sure Laiba's diapers and wipes are restocked at home. Check if we're running low on her baby formula too.
- Send the maid a quick reminder about Laiba's bedtime routine. She needs her storybook at **8 PM**, The Hungry Caterpillar—it helps settle her before bed.

Sayyeda's arrival:

- Ask Mufeed bhai to be at the airport sharp at 6 p.m. to avoid any delays in pickup.
- Remind Mufeed bhai to buy a couple of sandwiches and juice for her in case she's hungry after the long flight.

Work Tasks:

- Project report to Manager Ramesh is due by the end of this week. Need to find time to finalize it—perhaps tonight, once things quiet down.
- Draft the proposal for client Priya Sinha's new project on Sustainable Water Solutions. I'm already delayed. Will start tomorrow evening.
- Follow up with Rajesh on rescheduling the team meeting for next Wednesday.
- Finalize the task tracker for the client project. The team needs all updates by Monday morning.
- Email Finance regarding the billing dispute before Friday.

Health Reminders:

- I've been forgetting my own BP medication in all this mess. Need to refill by next week, at the latest.
- Check with Ammi's doctors tomorrow about the next steps—she seems stable, but I need a clearer picture of her recovery plan.

Make sure to note all the medications and any adjustments the doctor suggests.

- Confirm with Nurse Priya about the timing for Ammi's next CT scan and the physiotherapy session.

As she leafed through the pages of Bilal's diary, meticulously filled with every task, every reminder, every small detail, a quiet realization dawned on her. Relationships are not built on what we expect from the other person, but on understanding what they hold close and strive to protect. In our longing for grand gestures, we often overlook the subtle acts of kindness that silently weave beauty into our lives. Expressiveness, after all, has many forms. Sometimes it's not in words or displays, but in the quiet, unsung efforts—small acts of care that speak louder than any declaration. Bilal's love had always been there, steady and unspoken, tucked into the details of life, hidden in the spaces between his lists and responsibilities.

She realized now that affection doesn't always announce itself—it often moves quietly, without fanfare, holding things together in ways we don't always see.

As she read through the detailed notes, Sayyeda could almost see Bilal sitting there late at night, meticulously writing out everything. There was no room for his own feelings, no mention of his exhaustion or the toll this was taking on him. Instead, his focus was on her, the kids, and Ammi—making sure every detail was in place, ensuring that nothing slipped through the cracks.

The exhaustion on his face, the quiet resolve in his notes—it all spoke of a love so deep, so committed, that it made her chest tighten. She glanced back at Ammi's room. The sterile air of the hospital, the antiseptic smell, the constant beep of machines—it had all become their world now. But in the midst of it, Bilal was her anchor, holding it all together.

It was just like Bilal to carry so much weight without showing it, his love woven through these practical notes and lists. He hadn't forgotten a thing. Not about her, not about the children, and certainly not about keeping their world together, even as it threatened to fall apart.

She gently brushed her fingers over his hand, feeling the strain and the strength, and sat down beside him on the bench watching his chest rise and fall, matching the rhythm of the machines inside. And for the first time in days, she allowed herself to lean back, close her eyes, and rest. Not because everything was okay, but because at that moment, she knew they were in this together. They would carry on, together, just as they always had.

Rahim Tea Stall

1

Nizam Bhai pedaled slowly past the Engineering Canteen, his senses absorbing the familiar sights and sounds that had become woven into the fabric of his daily life. The students were scattered across the canteen like fragments of a dream—talking, laughing, some with their heads bent together over phones or notebooks, while others simply enjoyed the morning breeze. The air was cool, carrying with it the crispness of winter, and the sun, faintly warm, cast a gentle glow on everything it touched. It was the kind of morning that made you crave a cup of hot tea, and the students, with their casual joy, seemed to know this instinctively.

They sipped from steaming cups, some with plain tea, others with the aromatic sweetness of elaichi chai. Plates of patties and sandwiches were passed around, half-eaten samosas and parathas lay scattered on tables as the flow of conversation and laughter carried on. Boys and girls from every year—first, second, third, final—mingled together, their interactions unburdened by the academic hierarchies and gender stereotypes that so often marked other places. Here, they were just students, stealing moments of freedom between classes that didn't seem all that important in the grand scheme of things.

The canteen itself was alive with movement, a place with no fixed schedules, no set people, just a continuous ebb and flow of bodies coming and going as they pleased.

Bunking classes had become a kind of ritual, a norm that made it easier to drift in and out of the canteen without worry. The board hanging at the counter, listing the day's modest menu, swayed lightly in the breeze:

Plain Tea – Rs. 10

Elaichi Tea – Rs. 15

Veg Pattie – Rs. 20

Paneer Pattie – Rs. 30

Veg Sandwiches – Rs. 30

Samosa – Rs. 10

Aloo Paratha – Rs. 15

The menu wasn't extravagant, but it didn't need to be. For these students, these simple, inexpensive treats were the taste of college life—the patties shared with friends, the tea that warmed their hands on chilly mornings, the sandwiches that fueled endless conversations about everything and nothing. The canteen had a long list of savory delights, each one somehow a part of the shared experience, a part of the memories they would carry long after their college days had faded into the past.

As Nizam Bhai cycled forward, his attention was caught by a few students sitting on the stairs, textbooks open, scribbling hurried notes as they prepared for an upcoming test. It was a familiar sight, one that played out almost daily—students huddled together in a desperate last-minute attempt to cram formulas and concepts into their heads. In an engineering college, the sight of well-prepared students was rare; instead, you found frantic, last-minute revisions, and hurried discussions about how best to tackle the exam paper.

Some calculated how many marks they needed to scrape by, others scribbled notes to hide in their shoes or up their sleeves, preparing for the inevitable moment when desperation overtook caution. There were even a few who wrote formulas on their hands or scrawled equations on the back of calculators, hoping to cheat fate, if not the exam itself. And yet, if all else failed, there was always the elusive promise of improvement exams. Most students knew that these attempts to raise their grades rarely amounted to much, but the mere thought of getting a second chance brought a strange, calming sense of hope.

Some students paced back and forth, muttering formulas under their breath, while others sat in quiet clusters, heads bowed in concentration. It didn't matter that they probably wouldn't use half of this knowledge in the future—what mattered were these moments, the camaraderie, the shared panic and laughter, the collective experience of being on the edge, learning lessons about life that went far beyond the classroom.

Nizam Bhai's cycle wheels clicked softly as he continued to move, passing by the vehicle stand. There, bikes, scooters, a few cars, and even the occasional cycle were parked haphazardly, some crammed into tight spaces, others left on the side of the road. It wasn't an unusual sight—far from it. A decade ago, Nizam Bhai remembered, there had been no such luxury. Few students had bikes, and even fewer had cars. Back then, cycles were the primary mode of transport for most students, and those who could afford a motorcycle were considered fortunate. Even then, it was likely a hand-me-down from an elder sibling or borrowed from a father who could spare it.

As the years passed, Nizam Bhai had watched the vehicles grow more numerous, more advanced. Where there had once been rows of bicycles, there were now motorcycles, scooters, and cars. The change had been slow but steady, the signs of a world moving forward, even if he had remained the same.

Nizam Bhai's thoughts slowed as he approached a spot just outside the college boundary, a small, insignificant piece of ground that no one else seemed to notice. It was nothing more than a pavement with patches of overgrown grass, a few scraggly bushes, and an open drain that sent out a faint, unpleasant smell. The neem tree, old and sturdy, still stood tall, its trunk scarred by the engravings of students long gone—names carved into the bark, some with hearts and arrows, relics of young love. The ground was greasy, the soil having absorbed years of rain and moisture, and the remains of an old wooden structure lay crumbled, half-rotten, barely recognizable. Only a few nails and splinters of wood remained, most of it having been claimed by time and weather.

It wasn't much to look at, just a forgotten corner that most people passed without a second glance. But for Nizam Bhai, this spot held more significance than anyone could imagine. He slowed his cycle, something he often did when he reached this place. Sometimes he would stop altogether, just gazing at the ground, lost in thought. Other days, he would pedal by slowly, letting the memories linger. And on some days, when he was in a hurry or when the emotions felt too heavy, he would simply ride past, forcing himself not to look.

But no matter what, this spot was always with him. It had become a part of him, a silent marker of time. The spot where Nizam bhai stood, for 20 years, serving Mathri Omelette and chai.

2

"Maine bhi aapke saath chalna hai, Abbu," young Nizam eagerly pleaded, his eyes sparkling with enthusiasm as Rahim Bhai hoisted his daily baggage, preparing to set off for college. The morning sun cast a golden hue over the bustling neighborhood, and the sounds of vendors calling out their wares filled the air.

"Achha, theek hai Sattu. Ammi ko bata do," Rahim Bhai replied with a warm smile, his heart swelling with affection for his son. He loved these moments of connection, where the bond between father and son strengthened with every shared journey.

As they set off, Rahim Bhai pedaled his bicycle steadily, with Nizam perched on the front rod, gripping the handlebars tightly. The rhythmic sound of the bicycle wheels turning was a comforting backdrop as they navigated the lively streets. At the back of the cycle, a sturdy container held all the essentials: a gas stove, a jug of tap water, tea powder, milk, and sugar—everything needed to brew the beloved elixir of tea that brought people together.

Every evening, Rahim Bhai meticulously prepared for the next day, rising early to set up his humble tea counter before the students arrived. He would park his cycle under the expansive shade of a sprawling neem tree, which offered both relief from the harsh sun and a sense of community for those who gathered beneath its branches. The tree's broad leaves rustled gently in the breeze, creating a serene backdrop to the morning hustle.

As the sun climbed higher, students and teachers alike would pause their routines, drawn by the inviting aroma of freshly brewed tea. Some arrived clutching newspapers, eagerly scanning the pages for the latest headlines and stories, while others engaged in animated discussions about their classes and assignments. Nestled beside his bicycle, an old transistor radio rested on a small brick at the base of the tree, filling the air with a delightful mix of news, engaging radio shows, and timeless melodies that added a vibrant energy to the gathering.

Vividh Bharati, the most cherished radio channel of the time, often played Bollywood classics that enveloped the gathering in a warm embrace of nostalgia. The melodious tunes floated through the air, weaving a tapestry of memories for everyone present. Even professors, burdened by their busy schedules, would occasionally stop by to savor a song or two—a rare indulgence in a world where few owned a radio. Rahim Bhai considered himself fortunate, having received a second-hand radio from a neighbor who had upgraded to a new black-and-white television, a piece of technology that was a treasure in those days.

Young Nizam, with his innocent love for music, adored the enchanting songs of Kishore Kumar, Mohammad Rafi, and Lata Mangeshkar. His all-time favorite was Rafi's "Main zindagi ka saath nibhata chala gaya" from the film Hum Dono. "Jo mil gaya usi ko muqaddar samajh liya," he would hear his father hum, a tune intertwined with a valuable lesson.

"Whatever happens, always maintain your integrity. Imandari aur sabr, ye do usool hain zindagi ke. Inko hamesha pakad ke rakhna. Jo mile, usi mein khush rehna," Rahim Bhai would remind Nizam whenever the opportunity arose, his voice steady and full of conviction. With every word, he instilled in his son the profound importance of honesty and contentment, weaving a rich tapestry of values that Nizam would carry with him for years to come.

Evenings held a special charm for young Nizam, as the rush of customers dwindled and the world around them quieted down. These moments allowed Abbu to devote more time to his son, engaging in meaningful conversations that would become cherished memories. Sometimes, Rahim Bhai would slip Nizam a shiny 25 paise, a small treasure for the boy, who would dash off to buy some toffees from the nearby vendor, his eyes gleaming with delight.

On other evenings, they would sit together beneath the sprawling branches of the neem tree, where the fading light painted the sky in hues of orange and pink. Rahim Bhai would regale Nizam with stories of his past—the laughter and trials of his own childhood, the bittersweet memories of a nation in separation, and the historical battles that shaped their lives. He would speak fondly of his hometown, sharing tales of the friends he made, the mischief they got into, and the simple joys of growing up.

"Abbu, kaisa tha aapka bachpan?" Nizam would ask, his curiosity piqued.

Rahim Bhai would smile, lost in thought. "Woh din alag the, beta. Humare paas bahut kuch nahi tha, par hum khush the. Jab hum tumhari umar ke the, chidiyan udate the, aur khud bhi udne ki khwahish rakhte the," he would respond, his voice tinged with nostalgia. He would recount the early days of his marriage, the joy of welcoming Nizam into the world, and the struggle of setting up his business, which began in the modest confines of his own backyard.

"Abbu, mujhe bhi apki tarah chai bechni hai ek din, mujhe bahut maza aata hai sab logon ke beech," Nizam would exclaim eagerly, his eyes shining with dreams of the future.

"Bilkul beta. Balki tumhare liye to hum ek achhi si dukan banayenge, thode paise jama ho jayein, yahin neem ke ped ke neeche," his Abbu would respond, a mix of pride and hope in his voice. The thought of his son one day owning a proper stall, filled with the warmth and laughter that surrounded them, made Rahim Bhai's heart swell with optimism.

For people like Rahim Bhai and Nizam, saving even small amounts of money over the years became a labor of love. Each paise tucked away was a step closer to dreams that seemed just out of reach—a sturdy old bicycle, a reliable gas stove, or a warm blanket for the family. Setting up a proper stall felt like a distant dream, but witnessing Nizam's enthusiasm ignited a flicker of hope in Rahim Bhai's heart. He envisioned a day when his son would stand proudly behind a vibrant tea stall, serving customers with the same passion and joy that defined their evenings together beneath the neem tree.

3

The day was a moment of immense pride for Nizam, but even more so for Rahim Bhai. With age catching up, Rahim Bhai rarely visited the college campus now, his once agile frame slowed by time. It was Nizam, now a young adult, who had gracefully taken the reins from his father. He carried with him the same demeanor, the same authenticity, that had once defined Rahim Bhai. Nizam was meticulous in his routine—just like his father, he prepared everything the night before, ensuring that he arrived at the college early, before the humdrum of students began to fill the air.

Over the years, Nizam had made it his mission to maintain the same taste in the tea that his father had perfected. That consistency was vital; in the world of eateries, it wasn't just the quality that mattered—it was the memory of taste. The taste of tea was etched in the minds of the visitors, and whenever they experienced that same familiar flavor, it rekindled the emotions and memories of days gone by. Nizam was committed to preserving that bond. He even made sure to serve the tea in the same clay kulhad as his father had done. Nothing had changed. The aroma, the warmth, the taste—all remained the same.

The only thing that had changed was the stall itself. What was once just a bicycle with a container had now become a small wooden stall with a tin roof and a counter for the gas stove—a proper setup, just as Rahim Bhai had always envisioned. It had taken nearly a decade for the father-son duo to save enough from their modest daily earnings to afford the materials to build the little stall. Each rupee set aside was a step closer to this dream, a symbol of their shared perseverance.

Though his legs struggled to walk, Rahim Bhai couldn't miss this day. He came on a rickshaw, accompanied by his wife and younger son, who occasionally helped Nizam at the stall. Today, however, was no ordinary day. It was a day of celebration, a day to honor the years of hard work and dedication. Rahim Bhai's wife had even prepared gajar ka halwa for all the students who visited that day, a sweet gesture that turned the small tea stall into a place of warmth and festivity.

As the sun rose higher, students gathered around the new stall, their familiar faces lighting up at the sight of the beloved tea and the unexpected treat. It was a day to celebrate for the Rahim family, but more than anything, it was a day that belonged to Nizam—a day that marked his journey from a curious boy perched on the front rod of his father's bicycle to a young man carrying forward his family's legacy.

With quiet reverence, Nizam untied a small signboard from the cycle that had faithfully served them for so many years. He walked to the front of the new stall and hung the board with pride. It read, "Rahim Tea Stall." As the letters gleamed in the sunlight, Nizam glanced over at his father, who, though frail, smiled with a deep sense of fulfillment. His dream had come to life—not just in the wooden frame of the stall, but in the spirit and heart of his son.

The stall became famous in no time. Even in those days, branding worked wonders. Soon, "Rahim Bhai ke yahan chalte hain" became the go-to slogan for tea lovers around the campus. Students, teachers, and passersby flocked to Nizam's stall, drawn not just by the steaming cups of chai but by the sense of community that had grown around it.

Nizam, now fully in charge, continued to uphold his father's legacy with pride but added his own flair to the business.

One of Nizam's biggest innovations was introducing Mathri Omelette, a unique dish his mother had taught him long ago. Her method was different, a style perfected over the years. She would separate the egg whites from the yolks, stir the whites with finely chopped vegetables, and season it with spices like red chilies, cinnamon, black pepper, and a pinch of salt. A garnish of fresh hara dhaniya gave it a refreshing touch. Once the egg whites were cooked, she would gently pour the yolks over them, cooking them just enough to keep them slightly runny. The final touch was serving the Omelette with crispy, butter-toasted Mathris—a perfect breakfast for students on the go.

It didn't take long for the Mathri Omelette to become a sensation. Word spread quickly, and soon students from other colleges started to visit Rahim Tea Stall, eager to taste the now-famous breakfast. The small stall bustled with activity every morning, and managing so many visitors became challenging for Nizam, but he thrived on it. He loved meeting new faces and catching up with regulars, enjoying the endless stories that unfolded every day. His stall had become more than just a place for tea; it had become a hub for students to share their lives.

In that tiny 6-foot-by-6-foot stall, countless conversations took place. Some students shared how their day had gone, others spoke about their struggles—financial problems back home, or stories of heartbreak. Nazim listened, offering tea and quiet comfort in the midst of their hectic lives. Despite the cramped space, there was always room for everyone. Nizam brought in makeshift seating for his customers—used oil containers or discarded truck tires, turning the space into a DIY hangout spot that students loved. It was all so raw, so real—just like their own lives, a patchwork of small moments woven into a larger symphony of college life.

Each day, Nizam would leave home with excitement, looking forward to serving tea and hearing the stories of the students. Occasionally, he would bring Abbu to the stall, allowing his father to relive the old memories and see how their little tea business had grown into something much bigger than either of them could have imagined. Rahim Bhai, though weaker now, still beamed with pride each time he visited.

Nizam had his own quiet system for managing the day's earnings. He had four gullaks—clay piggy banks. One for his mother's household expenses, one for his father's medicines, one for Chhotu's school fees, and the last one for his own future—his dreams of getting married and starting a family. Whenever he spoke of the future, Nizam would say with a gleam in his eyes, "Ek din main bhi apne bete ko stall pe leke jaunga, jaise Abbu le jate the mujhe."

The legacy was alive, and Nizam was determined to pass it on.

As time spun forward, Rahim Tea Stall became the heart of campus life. It wasn't just a tea stall anymore; it had become the center of a thriving student food court. Other vendors soon set up shop nearby—Shabbir Bhai's fruit cart, Pandit Ji's chhole stand, Saleem Bhai's chowmein stall, Naeem Bhai's bhelpuri, and Jeetu Bhai's kulfi. Together, they created a vibrant marketplace where students could find a variety of snacks and meals. The whole area became a lively hangout spot, bustling with chatter and laughter. Friends gathered to enjoy their favorite dishes, and some boys even showed up just to check out the girls. There was a youthful energy that filled the air—light-hearted and carefree.

Many hostelers, often short on cash, would visit Nizam's stall, but even when they didn't have enough money, he never turned them away. Nizam always welcomed them warmly, offering tea on credit without hesitation. On some days, he would even treat them to a complimentary Mathri Omelette, a small gesture of kindness that made his stall feel like a home away from home.

The bonds formed at that humble tea stall were built on trust and mutual respect, without any formalities or conditions. It was a community bound together by more than just food—it was built on shared memories, kindness, and the small joys of everyday life.

In those moments, with the clink of cups and the hum of conversations, Rahim Tea Stall wasn't just a business—it was a living, breathing part of the students' lives. A place where stories were exchanged over cups of tea, and where people, young and old, found a sense of belonging.

4

"Nizam Bhai, uthiye, municipality wale aaye hain, bheed lagi hai stall pe," Chhotu's urgent voice broke through the early morning quiet, shaking his elder brother awake. Still groggy from a rare late night, Nizam Bhai sat up, rubbing his eyes, trying to process what Chhotu was saying. "Kya ho gaya?" he asked, his voice thick with sleep.

"Ap chal ke dekho, jaldi!" Chhotu urged, his voice full of worry.

Nizam quickly washed his face, didn't even bother to gather his usual supplies, and jumped on his cycle, pedaling swiftly towards the college. As he neared his tea stall, the sight of a large crowd—a mix of middle-aged men in formal attire, a few students, and his fellow stall owners—made his heart pound with anxiety. He pushed through the crowd, bisecting the sea of people until he was in the middle of the commotion. A senior municipal officer stood in the center, addressing the stall owners.

"Arey bhai, batayenge kya hua?" Nizam Bhai interrupted, looking around at the worried faces of his companions.

"Dekhiye Nizam Bhai, ye log keh rahe hain ke sab dukaane aur thele hatane padenge," Saleem Bhai cried out in distress.

"Kyun sahib, kya ho gaya?" Nizam asked the formal-looking man, his voice strained but respectful.

"Yeh sab bina permission ke laga rakha hai tum logon ne, aur ladkon ko barbad kar rahe ho. Cigarette aur jue ka adda bana diya hai tumne! Upar se orders aaye hain hatane ke," the man replied coldly, dismissing their years of hard work in one breath.

"Lekin sahib, hum toh salon se yahan hain," Nizam pleaded, his voice cracking with desperation.

"Toh kya yeh tumhare baap ki jagah hai? Hato yahan se, thodi der mein khali karane aa jayenge!" The official's final words stung Nizam like a slap. Without waiting for a response, the man walked away, escorted by his team, as they drove off in their ambassador car.

"Hum toh barbaad ho gaye, Nizam Bhai," Jeetu Bhai wept, despair in his voice.

"Arey nahin, koshish karte hain, bade afsar se baat karne ki," Nizam tried to reassure them, though he knew it was a slim hope.

"Koi fayda nahi hai," Pandit Ji chimed in, his face lined with defeat. "Yahan canteen ka tender lag gaya hai. Hum log ab inke liye zaroori nahi hain. Hamare rehne se inka business kharab hoga, isiliye yeh sab ilzaam laga rahe hain."

The students who had gathered around quickly rallied support, led by the union leader, and together with Nizam Bhai and the other stall owners, they marched to the municipality office to appeal. But every effort, every heartfelt plea, was met with rejection. The bureaucratic machine didn't care about the lives it was disrupting.

By the afternoon, under the scorching heat of the sun, Nizam Bhai and the other stall owners stood helpless as the municipality's cranes began demolishing their little food court. The vendors quickly salvaged what they could—thelewale dragged away their carts—but Nizam Bhai stood frozen, watching his world collapse. The crane swung, hitting the metal roof of his stall, sending it crashing to the ground. Panicked, Nizam rushed forward and grabbed the signboard that read "Rahim Tea Stall," clutching it to his chest as if it were his father's memory in physical form.

He didn't cry. He stood there, silently absorbing the destruction around him. The stall, the place where he and his father had poured years of effort, was now reduced to rubble. As the sun began to set, casting long shadows over the wreckage, Nizam Bhai remained rooted in place, his heart heavy, darker than the fading daylight.

That night, Nizam Bhai lay silently in his bed, the events of the day replaying in his mind like a never-ending nightmare. He hadn't eaten. He hadn't spoken. His two-year-old son, too young to understand, would never see the tea stall his father and grandfather had built with so much love and labor. His Abbu had passed away a couple of years ago, long before witnessing the destruction of the dream he had spun for his son. His mother, Chhotu, and his wife sat with him, offering silent comfort as the night crept on.

For months after the incident, Nizam withdrew from the world. He spent his days lying in bed, barely eating, sinking into a deep sadness. Sometimes, late at night, he would sit alone on the roof, staring at the sky, replaying memories of his father, the students who once filled the air with chatter, and the camaraderie of his fellow vendors. Everything had vanished in the blink of an eye. His hands no longer knew the comfort of brewing tea, and his heart no longer carried the same passion.

His fellow stall owners—Saleem Bhai, Jeetu Bhai, Pandit Ji—visited him often. They had found new spots in the city to set up their carts. "Ek dukan khali padi hai, wahin aa jaiye," Saleem Bhai would urge.

"Nahin, ab dil nahi hai," Nizam would reply, his voice empty. It was as if all the motivation, all the joy that had once defined him, had been stripped away. For the municipality officials, demolishing the stalls had been a routine task. But for Nizam, they had taken away his entire soul.

Then one morning, seemingly out of nowhere, Nizam woke up early. His wife, worried, watched him as he moved about the kitchen, gathering his things.

"Kya ho gaya aapko? Kahan ja rahe hain?" she asked, concerned with filling her voice.

Nizam paused for a moment, then turned to her and said, with quiet determination, "Mera beta chai nahi bechega. Woh padhega, aur vilayat jayega."

With that, he picked up his old cycle, loaded the few items he had left, and pedaled back into the city.

5

Nizam Bhai had grown older now, his once black beard now completely white, making him look strikingly similar to how his father, Rahim Bhai, had looked in his later years. The resemblance was uncanny, as if time had brought him full circle. Every day, Nizam bhai would wake up at the crack of dawn, just like he had for years. He would first drop his son off at school, then carefully gather his supplies for the day and head towards the city, setting up his shop at the new spot, away from the college campus.

Chhotu, his younger brother, had come of age and was doing well, having found work at a local tailoring shop. Nizam was proud of him, watching him carve out a future for himself just as they had done all those years ago with the tea stall.

But the city around them had changed drastically. The streets looked unfamiliar, lined with sleek new buildings, modern cafes, and upscale restaurants that catered to a different crowd. What had once been a small college town had evolved into a bustling hub, with trendy eateries popping up in every corner. The college students, who had once been the soul of the old Rahim Tea Stall, now flocked to these new places. The charm of the old, simple tea stall seemed to have faded for them, replaced by the allure of Wi-Fi, fancy lattes, and air-conditioned spaces.

The regular crowd at the new Rahim Tea Stall, now marked by the same worn-out board hanging proudly in the middle, had changed too. Gone were the days of bustling students and youthful chatter. Now, Nizam served tea mostly to a different kind of customer—some local office workers who stopped by on their way to or from work, a few villagers who would come to the city to run errands, and occasionally, a handful of students and hostelers who still preferred the comfort of his simple, warm tea over the fancy cafes.

Though the faces had changed, and the hustle of the college students had been replaced with quieter, more subdued visitors, Nizam bhai still ran the stall with the same dedication he had always shown. The tea still tasted the same, the kulhads were still used, and the atmosphere of the stall—though slower now—retained its essence. It wasn't just a business; it was a part of his life, a living memory of his father, Rahim Bhai, and the decades they had spent building something that had brought people together.

The morning crowd began to gather slowly, as Nizam Bhai went about the familiar motions of setting up his modest tea stall. His hands, worn and calloused from years of work, moved with a kind of steady rhythm, arranging cups, stirring the bubbling pot of chai, preparing for the day ahead. The smell of fresh tea leaves and the faint scent of roasted snacks began to mingle with the crisp winter air. A few rural men had already claimed their spots near the bench, their forms hunched under thick blankets, puffing bidis as they sat in a loose circle, absorbed in their own world of idle conversation. Their voices were low, their words punctuated by the occasional burst of laughter, their faces hidden behind clouds of bidi smoke and the bulk of their tattered blankets.

Nearby, the local dogs had begun to stir, stretching and yawning as they padded over to their usual place by the stall. They were a scruffy lot, but loyal to Nizam Bhai, knowing that before long he would toss them the stale Mathris left over from the day before. They waited patiently, tails wagging with the quiet hope of a few scraps to fill their bellies.

A couple of young men, dressed in office formals, hurried toward the stall, their shoes clicking against the pavement as they made a quick stop for tea before catching the bus to work. Their eyes were heavy with the weight of early mornings, but their conversation was light, punctuated by yawns and quick sips of chai, a brief pause before the rush of the day would sweep them away.

From the corner of his eye, Nizam Bhai noticed a figure passing by—an older woman, likely in her mid-40s, though the lines etched deep into her face made her appear older. She was wrapped in an old, faded blanket, her body hunched from years of wear and struggle. Her movements were slow, deliberate, as she extended her hand to the young men, her voice a soft plea for a few rupees. Her face was worn, but her eyes, half-covered by a loose scarf, were sharp with the practiced humility of someone who had spent years asking for kindness from strangers. She was part of the city's faceless roamers, people with no home, no anchor, moving through the streets in search of the smallest acts of charity.

Her life was reduced to the rhythm of the day—the quest for survival split into parts: morning, afternoon, evening. There was no future for people like her, no long-term plans. The present moment was all that mattered: finding enough to eat, making it through to the next hour, the next day. And yet, despite this relentless uncertainty, there was a strange sense of routine in her existence, a daily pilgrimage through the streets, her hand always outstretched, her voice always soft. At night, she would join others like her, huddling together for warmth, sharing stories of the day's encounters, sometimes using conversation as a distraction from the gnawing hunger in their stomachs.

But the young men ignored her. One of them waved her off without even looking, claiming he had no money, while the other shifted his gaze, pretending not to see her at all. The woman didn't argue, didn't beg any further. She simply continued down the street, moving toward other early risers in the hopes that one of them might spare a few coins or a bit of bread.

This area was different from the college campus where Nizam Bhai had spent so many years. The college spot had been full of life, but in a calmer, more intimate way. There, the students would sit for hours, enjoying the freedom that came with being young and unburdened by the real world. They would come in small groups, some taking breaks between classes, others skipping classes altogether, content to spend the day lounging by the stall. Space had always been limited, but the students never seemed to mind. They would make do with whatever they could find—a few bricks stacked together for seats, an old plastic stool, or even the back of a friend's cycle.

The drains at the college had always smelled faintly of sewage, a stench that should have bothered anyone passing by, but somehow it didn't. The students, having grown accustomed to it, barely noticed. Stray dogs and pigs, their bodies caked in mud, roamed freely, adding a strange kind of charm to the scene. It was imperfect, messy, and yet it was perfect for the students. In that chaos, they found their own rhythm, their own sense of belonging. They created memories in that space—shared laughter, stolen moments of quiet, conversations that would stay with them long after they left the campus. The dirt and grime became invisible in the glow of their youthful energy.

But here, in the heart of the city, everything felt different. There was noise—constant, unrelenting noise. The roads were wider, the drains were covered, and the vegetation was neatly trimmed, but none of it could bring the tranquility that had existed in the chaos of the college days. Here, life moved faster. People came and went, grabbing their morning tea or a quick snack before rushing off to work or errands. Their stay was brief, their purpose singular. There was no time to linger, no time to sit and share a laugh or lose oneself in conversation.

Nizam Bhai sensed the difference, but he didn't let it weigh on him. Life had its way of shifting paths, and this was where his journey had led him. Without hesitation, he poured another cup of tea, the steam rising in gentle spirals, warming the cool morning air. His hands moved with the same practiced ease they always had, even as the world around him had changed. With a quick swipe of his kurta's sleeve, he wiped the sweat from his brow and allowed a quiet smile to play on his lips as more customers drifted in, one after the other, filling the space with their chatter and presence.

"Sattu Bhai!" The voice cut through the early morning air, catching Nizam Bhai off guard. He looked up from his small tea stall, adjusting his worn-out glasses to focus on the two men approaching. Dressed comfortably—one in a track suit, the other in night pajamas and a jacket—their faces radiated an energy that stood out from the usual monotony of the stall. There was something familiar in the way they called out his name, a name few people around here knew. Not the "Nizam Bhai" the regulars called him by, but "Sattu Bhai," a name he hadn't heard in years. The memory of it stirred something deep within him.

For a moment, he squinted, his brow furrowing as he tried to recall who these men were. Their voices, their laughter—it all seemed vaguely familiar, like a distant echo from a time long gone. Then, like a flash, it came to him.

"Mehmood Bhaiya!" His face lit up, a broad grin spreading across his weathered features. He rushed out from behind his stall, trying to figure out how to greet them. Should he extend his hand? Offer a respectful nod? But before he could decide, both men wrapped him in warm, affectionate hugs, completely ignoring the sweat on his kurta or the dust that clung to his clothes. They didn't care about such things.

Their Honda City stood parked next to Nizam Bhai's old cycle, a symbol of the lives they had now, but also a reminder of the lives they once shared.

For these men, Nizam Bhai wasn't just a tea vendor. He was a piece of their past, a connection to the golden days of their college years. He was the man who had served them chai on countless afternoons, who had been there when their laughter and conversations filled the old campus spot. Time had passed, their lives had moved on, but the bond had not been forgotten.

"Kahaan hai aap log? Kitne saal ho gaye! Kidhar settle ho gaye?" Nizam Bhai's voice was thick with emotion, his eyes searching their faces, trying to reconcile the men standing before him with the college boys he once knew.

"Mehmood Bhai Australia mein hain, aur main Dubai mein," Danish replied with a grin, patting Nizam Bhai on the shoulder.

"Lekin aapke haath ki chai… kabhi kahin aur nahin mili!" Mehmood added, and the three of them burst into laughter, the kind of laughter that can only come from shared memories.

"Arey, abhi aap logon ke liye wahi special chai! Double patti, aur cheeni aadhi!" Nizam Bhai exclaimed, his heart swelling with pride and joy. He hurried back to his counter, his hands moving with a newfound swiftness, as if the years had rolled back.

The other orders were set aside; nothing was more important than preparing tea for these old friends. As he worked, he would glance over at them, catching bits of their conversation, hearing their laughter. He instructed his young helper, to manage the rest of the customers for the moment. Today, these men—his old college boys—deserved his full attention.

As the familiar scent of tea filled the air, it brought with it memories—of afternoons spent serving chai under the neem tree, of students huddled around his makeshift stall, sharing jokes, complaints, and dreams. He poured their tea into special kulhads, just like he used to back then, and alongside it, he placed a plate of Mathri and Omelette.

"Iska paisa hum nahin lenge… yeh hamari taraf se," he said softly, setting the tray down in front of them with a smile. The stall had changed—better seating, a more solid structure—but something about today felt different. There was an air of nostalgia, a warmth that came not from the tea, but from the memories these two men had brought with them.

As they sipped their tea and continued talking, Nizam Bhai stole glances at them, soaking in their presence. The past felt close again, almost tangible. For them, perhaps, it was just a brief visit, a stop on their way before they returned to their busy lives. But for Nizam Bhai, it was much more. It was a glimpse into a time long gone, a chapter of his life that had shaped not just the students who came and went, but him too.

Even after they left, after promising to return before heading back to their far-off homes, something lingered.

The Honda City had driven away, and his cycle still stood in its usual place, a small reminder of the distance between past and present. And yet, for a brief moment, the distance had closed. And that, for Nizam Bhai, was enough.

Nizam Bhai had no professional identity, no official recognition. He didn't exist on paper, nor was he part of any formal economy. All he had was an emotion, a memory tied to the heartbeats of the past. Long before the sandwiches, patties, samosas, and the varied menu that today's students indulge in, Nizam bhai served up the simplest of meals with the warmth of familiarity. But people like him have faded from the campus, becoming relics of a forgotten era, their presence now just a whisper in the winds of memory.

The current students likely remain unaware of their existence—those nameless men who once fueled the lives of so many students with their chai and small plates of snacks. Time has moved on, and so have the people. The students who once sat on rickety stools and leaned against the trees while sipping tea have now climbed the rungs of their careers. They've scattered across the globe, leading busy, successful lives.

Yet, for those like Nizam Bhai, life has remained suspended in that same daily grind, their existence unchanged as the world around them moved forward.

Each morning, he would mount his old cycle, the same one that had carried him for years, and peddle down the familiar road. The backdrop of the engineering college loomed in the distance, a place that had once been his world.

The scent of Mathri, Omelette, and tea wafted into the bustling street, mingling with the noise of honking cars and hurried footsteps. This new place lacked the laughter, the conversations, the camaraderie he once knew. Here, life was transactional, and he, just another vendor, lost in the chaos.

As the evening sun descended, Nizam bhai turned on his old transistor

"Jo kho gaya main usko bhulata chala gaya. Har fikr ko dhuein mein udata chala gaya"